# IS IT NIGHT
# OR DAY ?

# OTHER BOOKS YOU MAY ENJOY

# IS IT NIGHT OR DAY ?

FERN SCHUMER CHAPMAN

SQUARE
FISH

FARRAR STRAUS GIROUX

NEW YORK

SQUARE
FISH

An Imprint of Macmillan
175 Fifth Avenue
New York, NY 10010
mackids.com

Square Fish and the Square Fish logo are trademarks of Macmillan and
are used by Farrar Straus Giroux under license from Macmillan.

Square Fish books may be purchased for business or promotional use. For information on
bulk purchases, please contact the Macmillan Corporate and Premium Sales Department at
(800) 221-7945 x 5442 or by e-mail at specialmarkets@macmillan.com.

Library of Congress Cataloging-in-Publication Data
Chapman, Fern Schumer.
    Is it night or day? / Fern Schumer Chapman.
        p.   cm.
    Summary: In 1938, Edith Westerfeld, a young German Jew, is sent by her parents to
Chicago, Illinois, where she lives with an aunt and uncle and tries to assimilate into
American culture, while worrying about her parents and mourning the loss of
everything she has ever known. Based on the author's mother's experience, includes
an afterword about a little-known program that brought twelve hundred Jewish
children to safety during World War II.
    ISBN 978-1-250-04421-1 (paperback) / ISBN 978-1-4299-3413-8 (e-book)
    [1. Refugees, Jewish—Fiction.   2. Jews—Germany—Fiction.   3. Jews—United
States—Fiction.   4. Holocaust, Jewish (1939–1945)—Fiction.   5. World War,
1939–1945—Jews—Rescue—Fiction.   6. Chicago (Ill.)—History—20th century—
Fiction.]   I. Title.

PZ7.C3667 Is 2010        [Fic]—dc22

                                                            2008055602

Originally published in the United States by Farrar Straus Giroux
First Square Fish Edition: 2014
Book designed by Robbin Gourley
Square Fish logo designed by Filomena Tuosto

10  9  8  7  6  5  4  3

AR: 5.3  /  F&P: X  /  LEXILE: 810L

*For Tiddy's grandchildren*
*Ross, Keith, and Isabelle Chapman*
*Sam and Jake Schumer*

He who learns must suffer. And even in our sleep pain that cannot forget falls drop by drop upon the heart, and in our own despair, against our will, comes wisdom to us by the awful grace of God.

—Aeschylus
(c. 525–456 B.C.)

# CONTENTS

## AUTHOR'S NOTE

In 1938, my grandparents, sensing the growing anti-Semitism in Germany, sent my mother, Edith Westerfeld, to live in America, all by herself. She was only twelve years old. She was part of an American rescue operation later named "the One Thousand Children," which sought to place child refugees in foster families to escape Nazi persecution. The children knew little of what was happening to them, and my mother would not know her whole story until she was seventy-seven years old.

Giving voice to my mother and other Holocaust survivors has been a significant part of my life's work. In trying to understand my own identity, I have patched together my mother's story, bit by bit.

*Is It Night or Day?* is a work of historical fiction. In writing this novel, I have imagined my mother's voice and recounted some of her experiences, along with those of other children who escaped the Holocaust by coming to America.

# IS IT NIGHT OR DAY ?

# 1

## NOBODY TOLD ME ANYTHING

### Germany 1938

The first long train trip I ever took in Germany was my last. Now I see that it was a funeral procession. The mourners traveling with me were my father, my mother, and Mina, a Christian girl who lived with my family and was as dear to me as my big sister, Betty. We were burying my childhood.

The train would take us from our little town of Stockstadt am Rhein all the way to Bremen, about 320 kilometers (200 miles) away. Only once had I been so far away from home: a year earlier, my parents had borrowed our uncle's car, and we had taken Betty to the Bremen port to see her off when she left for America. Until then, I had never even ridden my bike farther than the next town. From that trip with Betty and from my geography class, I knew that Bremen was a big city, a port where huge ships came and went, day and night. Soon I would board one of those ships and sail to America, all by myself.

Chicago. I was going to Chicago, the city where Betty now lived with her new family. We had not studied *that* place in my geography class. But I knew from her address that Chicago was in a state called Illinois. I didn't even know what a state was, but I knew Illinois was in this distant place called America, which my father sometimes called *das gelobte Land*, "the promised land." It felt like I was going to the moon.

"Show me your passport." My father's voice broke through my thoughts as I stared out the train's window. The wheels screeched, steam puffing up off the tracks. Without taking my gaze from the window, I held up the passport dangling from a string around my neck. We all jerked backward as the train began to move. The local church, our school, my house on Rheinfeldstrasse, drifted past us, each a perfect postcard. The train picked up speed: the pictures blurred.

My father was still talking. "Now, Tiddy, your ticket is right here, too," he said, patting the breast pocket of his best wool coat. "You remember, we're sending a telegram to Onkel Jakob, your uncle in America. The Jewish group organizing the trip will let him know when to meet you. In Chicago, yes? Tiddy?"

Onkel Jakob? I'd never met Onkel Jakob. How would I know him when I saw him? I certainly couldn't ask anyone, since I couldn't speak English. And Onkel Jakob, who went to America nearly thirty years ago—would he still speak German?

I knew only one story about this *Onkel*, my father's eldest brother, who had emigrated in 1910. My father had told me that Jakob enlisted in the ambulance corps, not the infantry, in the United States Army. He feared that if he served in the infantry, he might find himself pointing a gun at the head of one of his two brothers serving on the German side.

His youngest brother, my father, Siegmund, was proud to have served the Fatherland in the Great War and proud of the medal he'd won—the famous Iron Cross, trimmed in white, with the year 1914 engraved on its face. Captured by the Russians and held as a prisoner of war, he learned to speak Russian. That made him fluent in five languages.

My father believed absolutely in Germany, and so he was stunned by the anti-Semitism that swept the country in the 1930s. "I can't believe my comrades would turn against me," he often muttered as he fingered the Iron Cross that was displayed on a bookshelf in our living room.

His ancestors—my ancestors—had been among the town's original settlers. The old records showed that the Westerfelds had lived in Stockstadt long before Germany was Germany, for more than two hundred years. My parents had told me that we were descended from refugees who had fled the Spanish Inquisition and settled—a few families here, a few families there—in the towns and cities of northern Europe. Only one other Jewish family, my mother's ancestors, came to Stockstadt. Their descendants, my mother's cousins, had fled to America a few years ago, when things started to get bad for Jews. After my parents sent my sister away, only four Jews—my mother, my father, my grandmother, and I—were left in the town of two thousand people.

I'd often heard my parents talk about how Hitler urged towns to make themselves "free of Jews." Now, a large sign in front of a village hall caught my eye as the train sped past. *Judenfrei,* it said. That town had met its goal.

But not in our town. In Stockstadt, there would still be three.

Why hadn't we all left together? Months, then years, had slipped away as my parents tried to decide what we should do. My mother wanted the whole family to emigrate together, but my father couldn't persuade his mother, who lived with us, to leave. In 1721, the Westerfelds had built our home, a large German Tudor held together with straw and manure, and carefully maintained and handed down from one generation to the next. My father's mother, Oma Sarah, often reminded us that this was her home; she had always lived within these walls, this town, this country.

"I was born a German," she would tell my father whenever he pressed her to leave, "and I will die a German."

My father wouldn't go without his mother. For the longest time, he thought that things eventually would change in Germany and, he'd say, things really weren't too bad. As long as the laws weren't too restrictive, as long as he could bring in money by buying and selling local produce, as long as he could believe that Hitler wouldn't last, he could wait. *"Der Vierer geht, aber der Fünfer kommt,"* he'd say: "The year '34 is going away, but '35 is coming." In German, it was a pun that suggested the Führer, Hitler, would be gone.

Still, my father didn't want to take any chances with his daughters. He and my mother debated endlessly, weighing my sister's and my safety in Germany against an unknown life in a foreign country without them. How could children survive thousands of miles away from their mother and father? He couldn't bear that thought, so he filed the papers for passports and permission for all of us to emigrate together, hoping that Oma Sarah, who never changed her mind about anything, might consider leaving the only home she and her Westerfeld ancestors ever knew.

The day my father nearly "died a German," he realized things were much worse than he had thought. He had gone to the tavern across the street from our house. Often, after work, he would have a beer with some of our

Stockstadt neighbors. As he walked in that evening, a group of rowdy men—many of them my father's customers, and some his grammar school classmates—were clanking beer steins and singing loudly. Several turned to face my father, stuck out their arms, and said "*Heil* Hitler," and burst into the Nazi national anthem, "Das Deutschlandlied."

My father, whom Betty and I called Vati, turned and left. But a few men followed, chasing him into our main street, Rheinfeldstrasse. He ducked into the stairwell at the village hall, hoping to lose them, but they saw where he went. He struggled, pushing against the glass door to keep it closed. The men counted together, *Eins, zwei, drei*, then heaved, shoving the door open. Vati was trapped. Calling him *dreckiger Jude*—"filthy Jew"—the men kicked and beat him until he lost consciousness.

Some time later—he had no idea how long—with swollen eyes, purplish lips, and a bloody nose dripping onto his blue-and-white-checked work shirt, he staggered through our front door, smelling of vomit and beer.

"Siegmund!" my mother shrieked, and ran to steady him. "*Was ist denn mit dir passiert?* What happened to you?"

For a month he lay in bed, recovering from broken ribs, bruised kidneys, and a ruptured spleen. Some days, it seemed he just lay there, staring out the bedroom window all day long. Finally, on the first day he was up and around again, he told my mother that he could see only one solution to the anti-Semitism in Germany. "We must send our daughters to safety in America."

I knew this only from what I saw and what I was able to piece together from bits of conversations I'd overheard. Nobody told me anything. Even when Betty left, no one said much; we behaved as if her trip were just a brief separation, a temporary inconvenience before we would all be together again in America. My parents could not bring themselves to speak of the possibility that we might never see one another again.

Betty was only fourteen then, but she seemed so much older to me. Just before she left, she had lost some of her baby fat, and her thick, dark hair framed her face, showing off her high cheekbones, clear skin, and beautiful brown eyes. I figured if I ever had to go to America, I'd be all right if I could live with Betty! When I told Vati this, he said that he couldn't necessarily arrange that. "We take what we can get, Tiddy."

Now they were sending me away and, though Betty and I would be in the same city, I was going to live with relatives, many miles from my sister, who was living with a foster family my parents and I didn't know. That family had agreed to take in Betty as a companion for their only daughter.

On the train, my father was saying, "When you get to Chicago, Tiddy, see how you might raise some money so that we can join you." Until recently, money hadn't been a problem for our family. But in the last few years it had become difficult for my father to make a living and he had spent most of his savings on passports, tickets, and bribes to get Betty and me out of Germany.

I turned to face him. "Your Onkel Jakob will help you send us the money," he continued.

I stared hard, scarcely listening, working instead to photograph my father's face in my mind, so I would always remember him. He was just forty-three, but he looked ancient. His deep brown eyes never sparkled anymore. It had been months since I'd seen the fine net of tiny wrinkles that appeared around his eyes when he smiled. And my mother—Mutti—I couldn't remember how she used to look. Young, I suppose. Nothing like the dead-eyed figure before me. These were people I knew, but barely recognized.

Once, we were the Westerfelds of Stockstadt, an old family completely accepted by the community. My father, a respected civic leader, had helped each of our neighbors at one time or another; no farmer had ever sold a crop without Siegmund Westerfeld's services. Every year of our young lives before the trouble started, Betty and I had gone to our neighbors' homes to help trim their Christmas trees; they would come light the menorah with us at Hanukkah and eat matzo at Passover.

All the neighbors helped one another out. When Mina was thirteen, she came to live with us because her family couldn't support all their seven children. She did chores around our house in exchange for free room and board. It was a loose arrangement and, as years passed, Mina became another sister to Betty and me. We even took a family portrait with all of us: Oma Sarah, Vati, Mutti, Betty, Mina, and me.

But now, suddenly, we were filth, Jews polluting the village. In 1935, the Nuremberg Laws cut us off completely, and after living in our town for more than two hundred years, the Westerfelds were no longer citizens. We couldn't vote, couldn't go to the theater or concerts or restaurants. We were still tolerated in the public school, but there were no more music lessons for Betty and me; Mr. Klaus, our mandolin teacher, told my father that even though Betty showed talent and he would have liked to work with her, he was not allowed to teach Jews anymore. Worse than that, Vati couldn't open his shop's doors to sell feed and supplies to the farmers.

Yet even then we didn't think of ourselves as Jews. We were Germans. I was young, and I didn't really understand how everything had changed, not till several weeks after Betty had gone to America—on my birthday, May 6, 1937, when I turned twelve.

We had always celebrated my birthday with a party; usually Betty, Mina, and the seven girls in my class came. This year, we sent out postcard invitations with a pretty drawing of four girlfriends seated at a formal table, all looking at the birthday girl. *Wirfreuen uns, wenn Ihr um vier Uhr zu einer schönen Tasse Kaffee zu uns kommt,* it said. "We will be happy for you to join us for a special coffee at four o'clock." My mother baked my favorite yellow cake with vanilla frosting. Mina and I set the table with our best tablecloth, napkins, and china.

Betty and I had created a special birthday ritual: the birthday girl always sat at the head of the table with her sister next to her on the right, in what we called *der Ehrensitz*, "the seat of honor." Every birthday I could remember, Betty was always there, right next to me, ready to help me blow out all the candles. But this year Betty was gone. I didn't want anyone else in her seat. Her chair would stay empty.

Long before four o'clock I was ready, wearing a new, pale pink party dress and a birthday hat. Through the front window, I eyed the brick pathway to the door, waiting for my first guest.

Mina, who was seventeen now, couldn't resist teasing me. "Tiddy," she said, giggling, "you're twelve years old! Try not to act like a six-year-old who can't wait for the party to start."

As four o'clock approached, Mutti busied herself making the traditional apple punch while Mina straightened the silverware and put a pitcher of milk on the table. Every few minutes, I jumped up to look out the window and see if anyone was at the door. After half an hour, I began to wonder if we had written the wrong time or date on the invitations. After forty-five minutes, I started to think: Had I done something that made all my friends mad? Finally, around five o'clock, I realized that nobody was coming. All the chairs, not just Betty's, would be empty.

As I took off my party hat and hung up my new pink dress, I began to understand. I hadn't changed, but everything around me had. Later that evening, Vati found me in my room, a lump on the bed, with one of Oma Sarah's handmade quilts over my head. I didn't want anyone to see my red eyes and swollen face.

"This isn't your fault, Tiddy," Vati said, trying to pull down the quilt. I wouldn't let him.

"But it's my birthday." I choked on my words from under the quilt.

"It's . . . it's Germany, Tiddy. It's all of Germany."

But he couldn't really explain it. No one could

One afternoon, shortly after my birthday, I went to the local movie theater. Betty and I had always gone to the movies on Sunday. After she left, I didn't like going by myself, and Mina rarely joined me because she had chores to do.

On this Sunday, Vati gave me ten pfennigs for the show

and insisted that I go. But when I got there, Mr. Lutz, the man who owned the small movie theater just two blocks from our house, wouldn't let me in.

"*Heute nicht, morgen nicht, nie, nie wieder.* Not today," he snapped, "Not tomorrow. Never, never again."

Tears filled my eyes. "Please, Mr. Lutz. Let me sneak in when it's dark, after the show starts." I couldn't imagine that he would say no. I often had babysat for his youngest daughter, Marie. "You can start the show and then open the door for me."

His cold, blue-eyed stare gave me little hope, but I kept trying. "I'll slip out through the side door before the lights come back on."

Mr. Lutz's face softened slightly.

"Nobody will see me, I promise," I pleaded, with what Vati called my puppy dog eyes.

I knew Mr. Lutz felt sorry for me. Every kid in town went to the Sunday afternoon movies.

"No one will know what you did," I whispered.

When he finally let me in, it was a double thrill. Not only did I get to see the movie, but in a small way, I, Tiddy Westerfeld, was beating the Nazis. For weeks afterward, I would tiptoe into the dark of the theater and sit alone at the far end of the very last row, watching the seven girls in my class, sitting together in the front row, laughing as they mimicked the actors on the screen. Not so long ago, I had sat there, too, laughing with them. When I looked away from my classmates and thought about what I was doing, my heart would pound so hard, I was sure someone would hear it. At any moment a Nazi in uniform might appear, the white in his armband glowing in the dark; someone would grab me by the elbow, call me a *dreckiger Jude*, and take me away.

Around this time, my parents started staying up late, studying maps, organizing piles of papers, and whispering on the phone (we had the first telephone in Stockstadt). Many nights they didn't even notice when I went to bed. My father now spent his days standing in line at consulates; at home my mother paced back and forth, sighing and crying.

"What's wrong, Mutti?" I would follow behind her, trying to get her attention.

"Nothing, nothing." She waved me away, as if shooing a fly.

"But why are you so upset?"

"Some things aren't for children to know, Tiddy."

But I knew.

Every Saturday at synagogue, the parents whispered, trying to keep details from the young. But that only made us more curious, and we listened more closely. And some things were hard to miss. Our congregation had always taken turns meeting in two neighboring towns, Erfelden and Biebesheim, because so few Jews lived throughout the area. Lately, someone had painted ugly anti-Jewish slogans on both synagogues' doors. Many of our friends spoke of Brownshirts—the Nazi police—blocking the entrances of their shops and preventing customers from entering, posting big signs that warned *Deutsche kauft nicht bei Juden*— "Germans don't buy from Jews."

Every week, at Hebrew School, the students were buzzing about what they'd seen or heard. Twice a week, I rode my bike to Rabbi Rubenstein's home in Crumstadt to study Hebrew with most of the Jewish children who lived in the neighboring villages.

One day, a fourteen-year-old boy, Friedrich Birn, said that his family, from a village across the river called Oppenheim, had been forced to abandon the home their family had built more than one hundred years ago. Now a Nazi officer's family had taken over their house—not buying it, just moving in—while the Birns were crammed, with a dozen relatives, into a one-bedroom basement apartment around the corner from their house. "I had to steal my own bike out of our shed," Friedrich said.

When the rabbi heard Friedrich's story, he said, "This is our history as Jews." Slowly, he roped us together by catching the eyes of each of the ten students in the room, and said, "Yet, no matter what happens, we endure."

Even though we were still living comfortably in our own house, a sign had gone up at our local swimming area: *Juden sind hier nicht erwünscht*—"Jews not wanted here."

As long as I could remember, every day of every summer Betty and I had gone there. It was a roped-off area of the Rhein River where all the kids would meet to swim, play games in and out of the water, race toy boats, and sunbathe. Once in a while, Vati would take us to the Rhein at sunrise for an early morning swim; he loved the water. But most days, Betty and I would get there in the late morning and not return home until dark. Our parents always knew where we were, and when they needed us, they'd come and get us there. Now it was off-limits—but only for me.

The summer after Betty had left, the sign went up, and Mina, my blue-eyed, blond friend, was outraged. She grabbed a shovel and dug like crazy in our backyard. Soon she had made a deep pit. After hours of lugging bucket after bucket of water from the pump to fill it, Mina announced, "This is our own swimming pool. If they won't let you go swimming in the Rhein, I won't go there either."

Still, on those Saturdays at temple, the adults looked more and more worried, then more and more scared. They spoke behind cupped hands, always asking the same question: "*Die Kinder! Was machen wir mit den Kindern?* The children! What will we do with the children?" Some parents shared information about organizations that might help, like the Kindertransport that arranged for thousands of children to go to England. I think my parents tried to place me in this program, but it was almost impossible to get a spot.

One Saturday morning as we walked to temple in Erfelden—we always walked to temple on the Sabbath, five miles or so each way, winter or summer—my father sternly warned my mother to gather information from the other parents while giving nothing away.

"We are all competing for the same few slots," he told her. "Find out what you can, but do not tell anyone our plans. We don't want to hurt our chances of getting Tiddy out."

By this time, it was unthinkable that we could organize exit papers so that all of us could leave Germany together. So many different approvals had to come through within a few weeks' time, and all these things cost lots of money in bribes. First, you had to have a sponsor in the country you were going to—someone who promised to help you get a job, so you would not become a burden to the government. Taking on a whole family was a big responsibility. Next, you needed a visa from the State Department or some other agency of the country where your sponsor lived. With visas in place, you then had to get an exit permit from the German government.

The hardest step, though, was the first: finding some country that would accept Jews. Our family thought about places I had never heard of—Argentina, Uruguay,

Paraguay, Cuba, Shanghai, Hong Kong—and, of course, Palestine and America. Our cousins' family, who had lived near us, in Worfelden, for two hundred years, had moved to Uruguay within the past year. I had never heard of the country before they moved; now the cousins were trying to arrange for our family to follow them there. Every so often, these relatives would send us airmail letters with colorful Uruguayan stamps of birds so strange-looking that I couldn't imagine they lived on this planet.

But Vati wasn't talking about our family moving to Uruguay anymore. In fact, after Betty left, Vati didn't say much about where we would go *together*. He had only one thing on his mind: getting each of us, any of us, out of Germany. He talked of nothing else, following every lead as if it were his full-time job.

Early one morning, I hurried off with him to the police presidium in the next town. A long line of hopeful people snaked along a hallway, down the stairs, out the door, and around the block, just to put their names on a list to apply for visas. My father wasn't the least bit surprised at the line; he said he had expected it. We didn't even get inside the building before the office closed, late in the afternoon.

That night, I overheard my father telling my mother that soldiers sometimes pulled people out of the lines and beat them right in front of everyone. I was never allowed to go with my father again.

———

The tighter the Nazis pulled the noose on all Jews, the more distant my mother became. One day Oma Sarah seemed especially worried about her. Now that I had no more friends, Oma Sarah and I played Parcheesi for hours. On this late summer day, the black and white buttons that we used as markers sat on the board, still in place from our game the day before. Oma Sarah was busy knitting. I begged her to play, but with a quick brush of her blue-veined hand, she said no. That really made me miss Betty. She loved Parcheesi, and I could always get her to play a game with me.

Late in the afternoon, Oma Sarah put down her knitting and pointed at me, then to herself, and then to the kitchen pantry. She wanted me to go into the pantry with her. That seemed odd, but I did as I was told. I was skinny enough to squeeze in between her bulky frame and the shelves loaded with jars of apples, pears, and prunes. It was warm in there and I felt a little dizzy, but the shelves smelled like our kitchen—a sweet, familiar mix of vanilla and cloves.

Then Oma Sarah's vinegary breath swept across me as she whispered, "For the next few days, follow your mother everywhere. Don't let her out of your sight."

I had no idea why this had become my assignment, but by now everything was strange. I didn't question my grandmother. I just nodded and slipped out of the pantry.

What was going on? If only Betty had been there! Maybe she could have told me.

Obeying Oma Sarah, I watched Mutti closely that first day. But soon I got bored, and on the third day, while I was tossing horseshoes in the garden, I suddenly sensed that Mutti was no longer near me. I looked around; she was gone. Frantic, I searched the house, the yard, even the pantry, everywhere. Finally, I went to the last place I could think of—the attic. That was where we dried herbs and flowers and hung sausages to age. There we kept things we couldn't fit into the house, all the furniture and books to be handed down from generation to generation.

No one but my father climbed up the rickety pull-down ladder in my parents' bedroom that led to the attic. Only once did Vati let Betty and me go up with him. We had been begging him to let us see what was there. When he agreed, Betty, even though she was short and round then, like Oma Sarah, charged up the old wooden ladder. But I was scared; it was unsteady, and I was afraid of heights. Betty called out, *"Baby, baby"* over and over again. I hated it when she teased me like that. I had to prove her wrong. My whole body shook, causing the ladder to shake, too, as slowly, without looking down, I willed my way to the top, promising myself with every step that I would never go up the ladder again.

Now I opened my parents' bedroom door and saw that

the ladder was down. My stomach dropped. Why would Mutti go up there?

Heart pounding, I climbed the ladder too fast to get scared. When I poked my head up above the floor, I saw that Mutti hadn't taken off her green gardening apron; the worn wooden handle of her favorite weeding tool stuck out of her front pocket. With hands blackened from dirt in the garden, she was adjusting a rope over a rafter. It dangled next to the large brown sausages my father had hung.

She didn't see me as I stepped into the corner of the attic. For several minutes I stood, barely breathing, a shadow watching her. For the first time, I realized that she didn't look anything like herself anymore. She was so thin now, and her face was more wrinkled than Oma Sarah's. The motherly warmth was gone from her deep brown eyes.

Yanking hard on the rope, she tested whether a fat knot she'd tied would hold. I could see a big loop at the end of the rope. *"Nazi Schweinehunde,"* she was mumbling over and over. I tried to speak, but no words came out.

Suddenly, when she noticed me, she jumped and dropped the rope.

"Don't follow me," she snapped.

"What are you doing?" Watching her, I felt sick to my stomach.

"Go away!" Her tone was so sharp that my eyes filled with tears.

"No."

I surprised myself; I wasn't allowed to say no to my mother. I sat down on an old wooden table, showing her that I wasn't about to move.

"I can't leave you," I said. "I'm not going anywhere without you."

But, of course, that's just what they made me do.

## 2

## ALL I COULD SEE WAS THE BLUE

At the dock in Bremen, we joined dozens of dazed travelers from all over Germany. No one seemed to know where we were supposed to go, or what we were supposed to do when we got there. How could we leave the only world we had ever known? Parents, brothers, sisters, grandparents, aunts and uncles and cousins—all were holding hands, clinging to one another, as if they'd never let go.

The place was swarming with Nazis, who wore the same mouse-gray uniforms with visor caps that made it impossible to see their faces.

*"Das reicht!* That is enough!" a Nazi barked at a woman holding tight to a sobbing little boy. They jumped away from each other, at least for the moment.

Looking around, I was starting to understand, *really*

understand, that I was leaving Mutti, Vati, Mina, and Oma Sarah . . . leaving all by myself.

My parents, like all those sending their children away, moved slowly, as if drugged with grief. That gray look on the parents' faces was as easy to spot as the cardboard tags their children were wearing. The ten or so of us children traveling alone had been given a large number to wear around our necks, and our suitcases were tagged with the same number. That way, neither would get lost. My number was 108.

As we passed huddled families waiting in long lines, I heard the word "America" spoken over and over, like the chant in a prayer. "We'll see you in America soon," parents were reassuring children. Every bit of conversation offered the same promise, ". . . in America."

In the building at the dock, long red, black, and white flags hung over our heads from the high ceiling, one swastika after another. *"Bewegt euch!"* someone in a Nazi uniform growled at us, "Keep moving!" Only the pigeons flapping up in the sooty skylights didn't flinch at their commands. I wished I could turn into a pigeon, free to fly home and stay there.

Besides, if I had been a pigeon, I wouldn't have had to lug this ugly brown suitcase. For the last two weeks, the suitcase sat wide open on the red chair in my bedroom. Vati carefully calculated exactly how much would fit in it, mindful that I had to be able to carry the suitcase myself. "We don't want it to weigh more than you," he tried to joke. I weighed only twenty-nine and a half kilos—about sixty-five pounds.

In the bedroom, I couldn't even look in the direction of the red chair. I had felt the same way a year earlier, when Betty was packing, but this time it was worse; we were sorting through *my* things and *I* was leaving. Soon, no one would be living in the bedroom Betty and I had shared all our years together. I wished Vati would take the suitcase back to the attic so I'd never have to look at it again.

Despite Vati's efforts, the suitcase finally did weigh almost as much as I did. My father had carried it as far as the train station, but as soon as we entered the building at the dock, a Nazi policeman came up to me and snapped, "*Nein, du musst es selbst tragen*. No, you have to carry it yourself." With eyes full of rage, my father stared at the man, then turned and handed the suitcase to me.

After we had stuffed the suitcase with every bit of clothing we could, my mother had wanted me to pack Arno in it, too. Arno was my favorite possession, a large floppy toy doll Mutti had made for my eighth birthday. I couldn't leave him behind, and I couldn't let him take this long trip shut away in darkness, where he couldn't be with me. So I carried Arno in one hand and pushed the suitcase forward with the other, as we shuffled in the long line to get my boarding pass. I inched along so slowly that people behind me complained. "*Geh doch! Beweg dich! Beeil dich!* Go on, move! Go already! Come on, hurry!"

What was their rush? Why should I hurry? If I dragged my feet, maybe I could postpone what I dreaded most. Every few minutes, the ship's foghorn blew a low, sad wail, like someone who can't stop crying. With each wail, I bit my lip and swallowed hard.

"What a great adventure this is for you, Tiddy," Mina said, taking Arno so I could use two hands to push the suitcase along in the line. "Just think—in ten days, you'll be in America. I wish I could go with you. You're so lucky."

Maybe if I had been older like Mina, I would have felt differently. But I would have given anything to be back in my bedroom with the suitcase open on the red chair. Here, everywhere I looked, I saw other ugly brown suitcases. Mine, held shut with two thick belts, wasn't big enough to hold everything I would need from home, but it was my one travel companion, the only thing I could take with me.

I didn't feel lucky at all.

Just then, a group of rowdy boys in the next line, all about my age and dressed in Hitler Youth uniforms, caught my eye. The boys back in Stockstadt—who wore brown jackets with leather buttons, black lederhosen, and red, black, and white Nazi armbands—had been marching around town for months, singing old German songs with ugly new words, threatening Mina and me. When one boy from my class learned that Mina lived at our house, he exploded. "Aaaakkk, Westerfelds," he said, and he spit on Mina's shoes.

Now I noticed the five uniformed boys were surrounding another boy who wasn't dressed anything like them. He was wearing street clothes and had a tag like mine around his neck. At first, I watched them uneasily, expecting the uniformed boys to bully the tagged boy. But then I saw them jab one another and the boy—in a friendly way, not mean at all—as if they had known each other all their lives.

"They'll probably be punished for this," Mina whispered.

"Who?"

"Those boys. They'll probably be punished by the Nazis for seeing a Jew off. Those *Schweinehunde*."

There was that word again. It means "pig-dog," and it was a terrible thing to say. It was the word my mother and Mina used to describe the Nazis, spitting out *Schweine* hard. Hearing Mina say it made me sad all over again. Even the way she said *Schweine* was Mina. How could I live without her?

Faking a sneeze, she said it again: "*Schweinehunde!*" I laughed, and then burst into tears. Not just for Mina, but for my mother, too.

Last night, when we had been sitting by the old wood-burning stove, my mother had said, "I feel so cold. I want you near me." I thought she was asking me to come to bed with her. I was confused; she never allowed that, not even when I had a nightmare. But I wanted to be near her, too. So I didn't ask permission from her or Vati. After she was in bed, Arno and I crawled in, curling up next to her, with my face against her soft cheek. I was hot, buried under several of Oma Sarah's quilts, but I didn't throw off the covers. Mutti's teeth chattered and her body shivered uncontrollably.

"*Ich liebe dich*. I love you," I thought I heard her whisper in a voice that didn't sound like hers. I wasn't sure I had heard her right; I couldn't remember that she had ever said that to me before. She stroked my hair with her shaky hand until I fell asleep.

But now, when I was about to board the ship, it seemed as if the night before had never happened. My mother seemed to be elsewhere, or worse, mad at me. Had I done something wrong?

"Where is your passport, Tiddy?" she asked sharply.

"Right here." Again, I held up the papers that hung from a second string, behind my 108 tag. She glanced at them, then shifted her attention to the top button that was loose on my gray wool coat, fastening and patting it securely in place. I could see that her hand was shaking.

"Do you remember how to fix this?" she asked, pressing the button hard against my collarbone. Mutti had given me a long sewing lesson just a week ago, teaching me how to tighten a button and do the hemstitch.

"I think so," I said, noticing that she wasn't really seeing me; she was looking through me, as if I weren't there anymore.

Slowly the line moved along and, at last, my father took my boarding pass from the ticket agent and held on to it for me. Waving his hand, the ticket agent directed us toward the dock where I was to board.

The four of us stood in the same spot where we had said goodbye to Betty a year earlier. It had been a drizzly March day, just like today. The heavy smell of the water, like rotten eggs, brought back the feeling I had had that day, when I could barely stand to look at my sister, knowing I wouldn't see her again for a long time. Now, a year later, I knew I'd see my sister soon in Chicago. But when would I see Mina and my parents?

I said to Mina what Betty had said to me when she was about to board the ship.

"I hate to leave you," I whispered, fighting my tears.

"It's best that you leave Germany now," Mina said. "Don't worry, I'll take care of your parents."

My parents! I could feel the color drain from my face. I hadn't even thought about them; I was worried only about myself. It hadn't occurred to me that my parents might need someone to take care of them. Who would know if Mutti went up to the attic again? Suddenly I felt sure I was going to throw up.

As we waited at the dock for the captain to remove the chains from the gangplank, Vati, who hadn't noticed that I was about to be sick, explained once again what I already knew: that I was going on this smaller ship to a huge ocean liner at a larger port.

"This ship takes you down the Weser River to Bremerhaven, where you will board the *Deutschland*," he said, talking much too fast. "That ship will take you to the North Sea, and then out to the Atlantic Ocean, so you can make the crossing to America. Yesterday, Tiddy, I was reading about the *Deutschland*—the ship you'll board in Bremerhaven. Tiddy?"

Nausea pounded through me, like the waves slamming against the dock. What if I threw up right here?

"That's half the population of Stockstadt—can you imagine? Tiddy?"

What was Vati saying? It seemed he was trying to talk to me about something, anything, in these last moments while he still had the chance. "But in thirty-six," he went on, "she was remodeled. Now she's one of the finest passenger ships making this crossing."

As my stomach settled a little, I had only one thought and a thousand questions. What if my parents didn't come to America? What if they never got their passports and papers? What if I never saw them again?

"Vati?"

"Now she carries nearly a thousand passengers on each ten-day trip."

"Vati!"

"Hmmm?"

"When do you think your papers will come?" I had asked that so many times during the past few weeks that he finally told me I couldn't ask him again. But I figured now he couldn't deny me anything.

"Uh . . . well, I don't really know." He had never said that before.

"Well," I said in surprise, "you must have some idea."

"We're close, we're close." He slipped into his usual answer. "We just need a few more things." I could have mouthed the words with him. "You must do what you can from America. Send money for the passage. Try to arrange for work for us. See if someone might sponsor us."

I never understood that part: How could a girl find a sponsor for her own parents? I didn't know anyone in America. Was I supposed to go up to strangers on the streets of Chicago and ask, *"Können Sie die Bürgschaft für meine Eltern leisten?* Can you sponsor my parents?"

The ship's horn gave a loud blast, a last call to say goodbye. Sisters, brothers, parents, and entire families moaned as they were ripped apart. Some of the children were trying to be brave, to hide their feelings. Some of the younger ones were screaming. Others, the older ones, looked worried.

"I know that you will do your best," my father said, handing me my boarding pass. "I know that you will make me proud of you."

"I'll try," I said automatically, but I didn't know what to do to make him proud. I kissed and hugged him, whispering, "I promise I'll try."

"And I promise I'll do what I can, Tiddy," Vati said, as a Nazi policeman, standing a few feet away, eyed us. "Now be a good girl." My father's face was so pale, it scared me.

Suddenly I couldn't wait to get on the boat. I didn't want to remember him that way. I turned to Mina and hugged her tight. Now even Mina, the toughest girl I'd ever known, was sobbing. "Tiddy, promise me you'll write every week," she choked, handing Arno back to me. "I'll be waiting for your letters."

And my mother—she wouldn't even look at me, staring instead just beyond my shoulder. She was gray   not pale, but gray, already fading into the color of the sky. Not saying a word, not making a sound, she kissed me on the forehead, and then brushed her hand on my cheek. I inhaled her familiar smell of onions, garlic, and soap, but her fingers were cold, colder than ice in winter. Then she turned me by the shoulders and gently pushed me onto the metal bridge.

I clutched the heavy suitcase in one hand and Arno in the other and slowly walked onto the gangplank, joining a crowd of passengers inching their way on board the ship. Then, when I got on the deck, I stood and looked back at my parents, feeling lost already.

No one came to tell me what to do, so I just stood there, waving. My parents and Mina waited and waited, never taking their eyes off me, but they didn't wave back. My arm started to hurt from all the waving, and after a while I wished the ship would just leave.

As I stood there, I heard the last words Vati said to me again. What he said wasn't as important as what he didn't say. He didn't promise me that we'd be together soon. He hadn't said a word about our future in America.

Suddenly, I noticed the people back on the dock were getting smaller. It looked as if I had stepped away from them, yet I hadn't moved my feet. The ship was moving.

Some of the parents standing on the shore collapsed, as if a bolt of lightning had struck them all at the same moment. Others fell to their knees, weeping and screaming like no adults I had ever seen.

My parents didn't move. They stood frozen, like people caught in an old photograph. As the ship picked up speed, moving down the river, the space between us grew wider and I watched as my parents and Mina got smaller and smaller.

A feeling of sadness rushed through me, starting in my

stomach, then spreading all over my body, making me heavy and dizzy. I was no longer inside myself; instead, I had left my body to watch the scene from above and I saw that nothing would ever be right again. My family was gone; my childhood was over.

My mouth opened. If I screamed, maybe everything would stop—the ship, the blue water, even Hitler. I opened my mouth wider, then as wide as I could, but nothing happened. I couldn't make a sound. I fell to my knees on the deck and clung to my parents with my eyes. I watched as they turned into tiny dots. Finally, they were nothing, dissolved in the distance.

Now, all I could see was the blue.

## *3*

## BUT I WANT TO GO TO THE ZOO

Maybe I fainted. Maybe not; maybe I just fell asleep right there on the deck. I don't remember.

I only know that somehow all of us got from the smaller boat to the *Deutschland*, and then set off on our real journey: ten days on the ocean.

I can see myself now, standing on the deck of that vast ocean liner on the endless sea, a dot on a dot on an enormous blue canvas. I remember I felt floppy, like Arno, whom I was surprised to find in my hand. I lifted him close to my face, as if I had never seen him before, and inhaled the smell of the wood-burning stove at home. I retched, sealing my lips to keep everything down. Arno, who had been with me forever, into whose little shirt I had wept when all my friends disappeared—now, all of a sudden, he was no comfort at all. He was home, and home was gone.

I dropped him on the deck. Then I unbuckled one belt

to open a corner of the suitcase and stuffed Arno in it. I tightly rebuckled the suitcase, sat down on it, and looked around. Just a few feet away, a chubby, moonfaced girl about my age was bent over a sobbing little boy.

"But I . . . I . . . I want to go . . . to go . . . to the . . . the . . . zoo," he gasped, gulping air between his words. "I want . . . want to see the . . . lions and the monkeys."

"You're *not* going to the zoo and you *won't* get to visit the animals," the girl said in a soft but firm voice. She seemed calm, and I found myself drawn to her. "But you will see other things that you can't even imagine. Skyscrapers, Central Park, the Statue of Liberty. It will be better than the zoo. I promise you. You will see America."

"But I . . . I don't want to go . . . to 'Merica." He stomped his feet. "I want to go to the . . . to the zoo."

I caught bits of other people's conversations. "You shouldn't have waved," someone said. I felt dizzy and mixed up, the way I sometimes felt when I got up to go to our outhouse in the middle of the night, not sure of where I was or where I was going. What a good thing I didn't have to go right now, I thought; I had no idea where to find the outhouse or whatever they called it on a ship.

"You shouldn't have waved!" A tall boy about my age, I realized, was talking to me.

"I saw you wave on the other boat when we left the dock. Didn't your parents tell you not to do that?"

"No," I said, suddenly panicked that I had done something awful. "They didn't tell me anything. Why weren't we supposed to wave?" Suddenly, my heart was pounding. Had I put my parents in some danger by waving? "Will my parents be okay? *Wird das meinen Eltern schaden?*"

"Yeah, I'm sure they are fine," he reassured me. Although I realized that he had no way of knowing, I wanted to believe him. "But you weren't supposed to wave." He stepped over to a pair of deck chairs. "Have a seat. And what's your name, *Fräulein?*" Vati was the only person who had ever called me *Fräulein*, and he only said it when he was mad at me.

I started to answer his question—then stopped. Suddenly, I didn't want to tell him that everyone called me by my nickname, Tiddy. That sounded too babyish, so I gave him my full name, Edith, pronouncing it the German way. "E-Edit," I said.

"E-Edit?" He smiled.

Then more firmly, I said, "Edith Westerfeld. What's your name?"

"Julius. Julius Biereg. I'm from Cologne," he said. "I mean, I *was* from Cologne. Where are you from . . . I mean where *did* you come from?"

"Stockstadt am Rhein, a little town south of Frankfurt." That's how my parents always identified our town.

"So didn't word get to your *little* town that you weren't supposed to wave?" he asked, with a bit of an edge, even though he was smiling.

"No." I didn't like his manner, but I was glad to have someone to talk to. Then I heard Oma Sarah's warning that I shouldn't talk to boys because I could end up in trouble. Well, I didn't see any harm in talking to Julius. Besides, Oma Sarah wasn't here to tell me what to do.

"Why weren't we supposed to wave?" I asked again.

"Everyone said don't wave goodbye. Someone might think you are heiling Hitler. You don't want to do that, do you? And didn't you hear the soldiers back at the railroad stations and the dock? They ordered everyone not to cry or show emotion."

Yes. He was right. I certainly had seen that at the Bremen dock.

"Julius?" A tall, attractive woman was calling across the deck. "Jules! Stay with us." She motioned for him to move closer. "I don't want to be looking for you all over the ship."

"Gotta go, E-Edit." He turned to me. "Now don't heil Hitler again, you understand me?" He smiled and stood up. Just before turning to go, he winked at me, the way Vati used to years ago.

I watched Julius join the tall woman, and a man, also tall, and a little girl. They must be his parents and sister, I thought, staring as his mother whispered into his ear. I heard my mother whisper what she had said to me last night. It sounded like *Ich liebe dich*—"I love you"—but I couldn't be sure. I should have told her that I loved her. Why hadn't I said something when I had the chance?

Sometimes, at home, my mother's voice irritated me, especially when she listed the chores she expected me to do each day. But now I would have given anything to hear that list. Already, I barely remembered the sound of her voice. Panic gripped me. How would I hold on to her if I couldn't even hear her voice anymore? I had promised myself that I would keep her close to me by playing in my mind the things she always said—like a recording—over and over again. She had last spoken to me only that morning, but I could feel her fading as each minute passed. Was I losing her?

My mind filled with questions. Why couldn't my parents be on this ship with me? Other families had left Germany together; they were all around me. But Oma Sarah had refused to leave, and that was that. That was why my parents said they couldn't come with me. I resented Oma Sarah for choosing her home over her family. Now I couldn't stop myself from thinking what I had never dared to think before. Did my parents love Oma Sarah more than they loved me? The thought would not go away. Would they really come to America? Or had they just said that so I would cooperate? Did they just send me away to get rid of me?

When I worried like this, I thought about how I behaved at home, making a list in my mind of the things I did that irritated my parents. Yes, I never ate all my dinner, which Vati said was wasteful. I was known for "getting lost" on the way home from an errand; I'd go to the bakery or the store and get sidetracked by the sun sparkles that I called stars on the Rhein River, or by the brightness of the green trees against the blue-and-white afternoon sky. Once, Oma Sarah caught me cleaning the henhouse, feeding the chickens, and collecting the hens' eggs on the Sabbath. She was upset because we weren't supposed to work on Saturdays, but I worried that the chickens might go hungry.

Still, I didn't think any of these misdeeds were enough to make my parents want to get rid of me. But then again, if they expected to see me soon, why had they spent the past few weeks teaching me how to live on my own? Everything had happened so quickly; we'd heard only three weeks ago that my papers were in order so that I could leave Germany and be allowed into America. As soon as she got the news, Mutti made me two smocked blouses and hired a local dressmaker to provide three dresses and a skirt. It was expensive and I felt guilty. Maybe she thought she wouldn't be spending money on me after I left. Maybe never again.

But then, when I had asked my mother for photographs of her and my father, she'd said: "You won't need them. We'll see each other soon enough in America." So she only packed a couple of passport photos. The pictures were small and hardly looked like my mother and father. Their faces were so unhappy and old-looking, all tense and worried. Now the tiny passport pictures were all I had of them.

During the past three weeks, my parents had hurried to give me a lifetime of instruction and guidance. My father talked to me about money, telling me over and over that I should find a way in America to help the rest of the family leave Germany. He was confident that a smart girl like me would think of something, but I wasn't so sure.

My mother explained how a girl's body changes as she becomes a woman. Then she stuffed one of her old ivory-colored camisoles with tucks—what she wore as a bra—into my suitcase. I couldn't imagine my skinny body ever needing the camisole.

Even Oma Sarah had given me a clumsy, serious lecture as she was teaching me how to knit. "You know, you must be very careful when you spend time with boys," she said. "No, the needle goes in the front and under to knit. You're doing a purl stitch." She took the knitting from my hands to fix the stitch. "They often take advantage of girls, you know."

"Who?" I asked as she handed the knitting back to me.

"Boys. Bring the yarn around the needle from the back. When you purl, it goes around the front."

"Oh, now I get it. But I can't work the yarn around my finger the way you do." She slipped the yarn around the needle so quickly I could hardly follow the action.

"Years of practice, *meine liebe.* You'll get there. You must

42

stay with it. And with knitting, you always have something to do."

Then, without looking me in the eye, she whispered: "They like to touch you. And you have to be careful, because you can end up in trouble."

"In trouble?" Confused, I dropped a stitch. I'm in trouble right here, I thought, handing my knitting back to Oma so she could straighten it out.

"Always remember, you have to be careful. In, around, through, and out."

My mother found room in my suitcase for a big supply of bleached white rags to use as cloth sanitary napkins, even though I didn't even have my monthly period yet. She must have thought it would happen before she saw me again. That could be a year or two or . . . who knows. I sighed, weighing all these details to figure out what my parents knew and whether this information could tell me when they might show up in America.

"Which camp are you going to?" The round, redheaded girl who had been comforting the little boy was now talking to me. As she came closer to me, I saw that she had a sprinkling of freckles across her nose.

"What?"

"Which camp are you going to?" she asked again, emphasizing the word "camp."

"Camp? Concentration camp?" I asked, stunned. I didn't know what a concentration camp was, but I had heard the grownups at synagogue hush when those words were spoken.

"No, not those," she said, suddenly looking frightened. "Those are only in Europe. We're going to fun camps, for tennis and swimming and games. I'm going to one in a city called . . . I think it's called *Zay*-attle, on the other side of the country. At least, that's what my parents said. They told me I will have so much fun hiking and horseback riding."

"Well, I didn't hear anything about going to camp," I said, thinking that camps would explain why I'd seen a girl carrying a wooden tennis racket. "All I know is that I'm going to Chicago to live with my Onkel Jakob and Aunt Mildred. They're going to meet me at the train station in Chicago."

"Really," the girl said. "I'm not sure who is going to meet me. Maybe the camp counselors." She searched my face, as if she hoped that I would reassure her in some way. Then she looked down, placed a hand on her stomach, and added, "I don't feel so good."

"What's wrong?" Now I was the one trying to comfort her. The little boy she had been mothering was piled in a miserable heap on the deck, red-faced and exhausted, moaning, "The zoo . . . the zoo." A young woman leaned over his crumpled body and said softly, "*Es ist in Ordnung. Es ist in Ordnung.* It's okay. It's okay." But he didn't even look up at her.

"My stomach feels funny," the girl said, and I was a little scared to see how pale she had gotten—almost gray. "And I'm really cold." I looked across the water as far as I could see. There was no land anywhere now; the ship was rolling with the waves, rocking from side to side, in a steady, sickening rhythm. As the sun began to set in stripes of deep colors to the west, the wind picked up, slapping our faces.

"I think I should go lie down in the berth," the girl said.

"Do you want me to come with you?" I asked, eager to get out of the cold myself.

"Yeah, come with me." She grabbed my elbow. "What cabin are you in?"

"I don't know."

"It's on your boarding pass," she said.

I looked and found the number. "I'm in cabin two two three."

"Really? So am I. With two older girls. Liesel—she's around fifteen, I think—is from Heidelberg. And the escort for all of us children traveling alone is Franzi. You saw her, the lady who was talking to the crying boy? She's nineteen, and not even Jewish! They both seem nice."

"What's your name?" I asked.

"Gertie. Gertie Katz. What's yours?"

"Tid . . . E . . . Edith Westerfeld."

Dragging my suitcase over to the spiral staircase that led to the lower deck, I noticed the collapsed little boy finally had fallen asleep on the deck. The escort had placed a pillow under his head and let him stay in that spot.

"I feel sorry for him," Gertie whispered as we approached the boy. "He's from my hometown, Waldheim, but I don't even know his first name. He is the younger brother of my classmate Ruth Schifter. I mean . . . she was my classmate. She was sent to England last month."

The boy's tear-streaked face was puffy, and his pink mouth was open in an O, as if he were still begging to go to the zoo. I felt for him . . . and for me.

I tried to breathe deeply to calm myself down. I couldn't push the air into my lungs. I tried again. Now I was gasping, but still the air didn't reach me. *Und noch einmal.* And again, I gulped and gasped for the air I couldn't get. Could someone drown without even being in the water? *Und noch einmal.* Breathing shouldn't be something that I had to think about. *Und noch einmal.* I worried I might suffocate.

I remembered one other time I had this feeling. It was an afternoon in the fall, when I took a walk with my parents at the Kühkopf, a nature area near our home. I was nine years old, I guess, and I walked ahead of them on an overgrown dirt path, looking for wild peacocks.

I thought my parents were right behind me. But when I turned around, they were gone. I took several steps back the way I came.

"Vati? Mutti?"

No answer.

"Vati!" I called.

They must have gone off in another direction. It was getting dark. I stood still, holding my breath to listen for someone rustling in the brush. Then, when I drew a breath, the air didn't reach my lungs. I had to tell myself, *Atme*, "breathe." I spotted them both a few minutes later. But now, once again, my head pounded and my heart raced.

How could they have left me alone?

# 4

## SEASICK

On our second full day on the *Deutschland*, Julius and another boy banged on the door of our cabin right after breakfast. Gertie opened the door just a crack, and both boys stuck their heads into our tiny third-class cabin. With four bunk beds, a washstand, and a large wardrobe, the room, if you could call it that, was so small that a person could hardly turn around in it.

Liesel was still in bed. She was so sick that Franzi, our escort, stayed with her all the time, except when she went to check on the boy who wanted to go to the zoo. It had taken Franzi more than an hour on that first night to persuade him to go to sleep in his cabin.

"Peter and I were wondering . . ." Julius kept his hand on the door to prop it open. "Do you want to explore? We could poke around the ship."

"They won't let kids snoop," the other boy said.

On our first day on board, we had discovered that the adults took it upon themselves to keep those of us traveling alone in line. When any of us would run past them on the deck, occasionally bumping into their chairs, someone would yell at us: "*Langsam! Langsam! Lauft nicht so schnell!* Slow down!" Or "Don't run!" Or "Where are you going in such a hurry?"

Obviously, nowhere. There was nowhere to go.

We looked at one another, trying to figure out what we could do. "I have an idea!" Julius's face lit up. "Sounds kind of silly, but let's play hide-and-seek . . ."

"Yeah, great idea!" Peter talked over Julius, finishing his sentence. "That way, we can explore the ship at the same time."

"But don't run," Julius said, raising his flat hand like a stop sign, "or the deck gestapo will get you."

A chorus of "Not it!" rang out. I didn't think fast enough to speak up, so I was it.

But I didn't mind, as long as I wasn't alone. Most of us—that is, the ten children traveling without parents—clung to one another. Only the little boy who wanted to go to the zoo kept to himself.

Within the first few hours of the journey, we had paired off. Soon we said our names together, as if they were one. Gertie and I became EdithandGertie. Even Julius, who was traveling with his family, had become part of one name, JuliusandPeter. Julius stuck with our group all the time, returning to his parents only when they insisted he eat meals with them or sleep in their cabin. The two boys were an odd match. Peter was probably a year or two older, yet he looked and acted younger than Julius. Julius was cool and quick to make a joke, while Peter was shy and awkward.

*Achtundneunzig, neunundneunzig, hundert.* Ninety-eight, ninety-nine, one hundred. "*Fertig oder nicht, ich komme jetzt.* Ready or not," I shouted, "here I come!"

I looked up and caught the eye of a steward walking by. The sight of him made me stop instantly. He was wearing a blazer decorated with a swastika. Back home, I was used to seeing swastikas everywhere, and of course the *Deutschland* was a German ship. But as I stared at that sickening emblem, anger flooded through me; I could feel my face turn red. These Nazis had taken over everything—my home, my village, my country. They had made my parents send me away. And now here they were still, running everything.

The steward's icy blue eyes followed me. I shivered, my anger turning into fear.

"Edith," one of the boys called out from his hiding place. Probably Peter, I thought, turning back to our game.

"Ready or not," I cried out, as I started down the deck, where dozens of passengers were sitting or standing against the rail. Some were Jewish families emigrating together. Several young men dressed in tailored German suits were traveling together, too; I overheard one of them talking about going to a university in New Jersey to study mathematics. Well-dressed, wealthy-looking American couples were stretched out on the deck chairs with plaid wool blankets covering their knees, the men smoking cigars and the ladies drinking coffee as they laughed and chatted in English.

I tried not to bother the adults as I poked behind empty deck chairs, circled posts, and opened closet doors, searching for my friends. Finally, I spied Gertie under the commander's bridge.

"Got you!" I said, a little too loud. A couple of the ladies squinted at us, then raised their eyebrows disapprovingly.

"Ah, I knew it was too easy." Gertie sounded disappointed, but I wondered if she had made it easy so we wouldn't be separated for long. She followed me as we looked for the others. We came upon the ship's boutique—an elegant shop we weren't allowed to enter—and together we gazed at a mannequin in the window, dressed in a fancy copper-colored jacket, fitted skirt, and an elegant, brimmed hat.

"Some day in America," Gertie said, "I'm going to dress just like that."

I couldn't imagine plump little Gertie in one of those narrow skirts. I wondered if she—or I—would ever be old enough or rich enough to dress in such fine things.

Eventually we spotted Peter behind a deck chair. Tiring of the game, I begged him for a clue about Julius's hiding place. He pointed downstairs, toward the engines.

I hurried down the spiral steps belowdecks, past a "No Admittance" sign. At last, I spied Julius, who had found the perfect hiding spot: a cubbyhole near the machine rooms on the lower deck.

"Aha, there you are!"

"Finally!" His blue eyes beamed up at me as he stretched his legs. "I was getting tired of waiting for you."

"I didn't think we were allowed to be here."

"I'm not sure we are." He laughed, then pointed to a bench away from the noise. "Here, have a seat."

No boy had ever asked me to sit with him. The boys at home never said anything to me, except to make fun of me for being Jewish.

"So what's Stockstadt like?" Julius sat so close that his knees were almost touching mine. "I've never heard of it."

"Uh, well." I felt my face getting red again. I didn't really know how to talk to a boy, so I asked a question instead. "What's Cologne like?"

Julius smiled, his teeth as white as fresh snow. "Cologne's a big city, very old, with a huge train station and a cathedral with tall spires that took over six hundred years to build. That's what it's famous for. What's Stockstadt famous for?"

I remembered learning about Cologne's cathedral at school. But I couldn't think of anything special about Stockstadt.

"I don't know." What could I tell him? That all the houses are built on stilts because the river floods so often? That's why they call it Stockstadt. It means "town on stilts."

Instead, I found myself saying, "Stockstadt is right on the Rhein River. A ferry goes across the river, so you can go from the village to the Kühkopf. We often go there on Sunday. I mean, we used to go . . ."

"So where are you going in *America?*" he asked.

"Chicago," I said.

"Really?" His eyes widened as he smiled broadly. "Me, too."

"I'm going to live with my aunt and uncle there," I explained, adding the one thing I knew about their American life that I thought would impress him: "They live in an apartment with *indoor* plumbing."

Julius laughed. "My father is going to work for some of Al Capone's boys . . . you know, the Chicago gangsters." A smile played at the corner of his lips.

"Really?"

"Yeah," he said with a straight face. But then he couldn't hold it. "Actually, he's going to referee the rematch of the Max Schmeling–Joe Louis heavyweight fight."

"Nooooo." I shook my head, certain that he was making that up, too.

"Okay, okay, okay." Julius laughed. "My father *is* Max Schmeling."

"Oh, come on."

"Okay." Julius changed his tone. "He got a job as a professor at a university in Chicago."

"That, I believe." His father looked like a professor, with short gray hair, a closely trimmed beard, and wire-rimmed glasses—a little like Vati, except for the beard.

Julius studied my face and looked at me as if he wanted to say something, but didn't know if he should. "Why didn't your parents leave Germany with you?"

His question brought back all the heaviness. I looked down at my lap. How could I explain to him something I didn't understand myself? His family was right here with him. He was not frightened and alone. He still had his own world.

Tears spotted the new red cotton blouse that Mutti had made me. Julius touched the embroidered flowers on my blouse as he gently placed his arm around my shoulder. I let out a deep breath. He had his own smell, a mixture of sweat and soap. In that moment, I felt something I had never known before—comfort and thrill at the same time.

"You can have supper with my family, if you'd like," he

whispered, squeezing my shoulder. Then he stood up and bowed slightly. "Promptly at noon any afternoon this week, *Fräulein!*" he said with such a funny upper-crust accent. In spite of my tears, I laughed.

On our first morning on the *Deutschland*, Gertie and I had gone looking for breakfast at eight o'clock sharp. "You are much too early," a gruff steward snapped. But we had been told the night before that breakfast was served at eight o'clock.

A passenger sitting nearby looked up from reading the *Deutschland*'s daily newspaper, which featured the day's menu and daily activities on board the ship. "Even though your watch says it's eight o'clock and time for breakfast," he explained, "here at sea it is only seven o'clock. We've already passed through one time zone. Each day for the next six days, the ship's clock will be set back another hour."

We nodded, but we didn't completely understand. I wished Vati had been there to explain it to me. Gertie and I went back to our berths and dozed until we heard the wake-up call—the familiar German song "Trompeter von Säckingen." That meant it was eight o'clock ship's time, and breakfast was served. We raced back to the deck again.

Our breakfast was luxurious: fried eggs, fat little bread rolls with sausage, fresh fruit, and lots of tea. Gertie ate four eggs—she counted—because her family hadn't had any in months. After breakfast, everyone was served an orange. Gertie immediately tucked hers away in the pocket of her red sweater, creating a bulge that was noticeable for the entire journey. She could have had a fresh orange every day, but she held on to that one . . . just in case.

For me, none of the food had any taste. I liked looking at it, but I never felt like eating. Oranges, sugar, even chocolate—all the things I had craved at home—were plentiful here on the ship. Yet none of the food could fill my emptiness. If I couldn't share food with the people I loved, if *they* couldn't have eggs and chocolate and bright, juicy oranges, I wouldn't either. I felt empty inside, but never hungry.

I was reminded constantly of that hollow feeling, because meals were a big part of our days on the *Deutschland*. First, of course, was breakfast; then, at midmorning, the stewards brought out trays with cups of steaming hot bouillon served with crisp pretzels for a snack. Just like at home, the big meal was served in the middle of the day. The stewards might pass platters of sliced roast beef, or chicken with rice, or maybe duck, lamb, or veal. Big bowls filled with potatoes and cabbage were offered, and sometimes green beans or beets or peas, too. Often there was a salad of fresh vegetables: cucumbers, lettuce or cabbage, carrots, and even tomatoes. At home, fresh vegetables were a rarity, even during the summer. Oma Sarah believed in cooking or jarring everything, and Mutti never disagreed.

At every meal, the stewards offered slices of a rich, yellow braided bread that reminded me of the challah Mutti made on Fridays. And each day seemed like a special occasion because we always had dessert. So many different kinds! Ice cream in three flavors, crisp little fritters, cookies and cakes, fruit compote, and chocolate and vanilla puddings with thick fruit sauce. We drank tea or hot cocoa or coffee, with as much cream as we liked. Then, at five o'clock, the stewards again blew the trumpet to call the passengers to tea and zwieback—toasted crackers that reminded me of home. Finally, in the evening, there was a supper of all kinds of sausages, cheeses, and bread.

Meal after meal, I left the food on my plate untouched. The other children rushed to the table, excited to taste the fruits, meat, and desserts that they hadn't had in months or even years. But for me, nothing was tempting.

Nothing except ice cream. The stewards would give passengers ice cream at any time of the day, just for asking. At first, we didn't know what it was. We had never seen this American food before, and some passengers even tried to spread the "frozen butter" on bread.

I didn't know whether I should eat it. What if it made me seasick? Only when I saw Julius and Peter gobbling it down did I decide it must be all right.

Once I started, I couldn't stop. I felt as if I had an ache

or a hole in my belly that could only be filled with the cool, creamy taste of chocolate or vanilla or strawberry. To tell the truth, whether I licked an ice cream cone or spooned it from a cup, I could barely tell one flavor from another.

Still, I craved it. The hole grew deeper. I had to fill it.

Some days, I felt guilty that I was eating such a treat without Mina or my family. But even that didn't get in my way. Often I ate so much ice cream in the afternoon that I would spend the evening in our cabin, only running out to the deck to throw up.

"You're seasick, Edith," the chaperone Franzi said when I returned. "Come lie down and I'll sit with you and Liesel." She patted my berth and fluffed my duvet—a puffy blanket that wasn't nearly as soft and warm as the ones we had on every bed at home.

"No, thanks," I said. "I'll be fine." I didn't want to take Franzi away from Liesel. Besides, I knew I had brought on my own "seasickness." I knew how to stop it, but I couldn't.

One day I joined Julius and his family for the noon meal. Only a few hours earlier, I had eaten six ice creams at breakfast. So I pushed my roast lamb, red potatoes, and cooked carrots around on my plate, hoping no one would notice I hadn't taken a bite.

I was wrong about that. "*Du ißt wie ein Vögelchen*. You eat like a bird!" Frau Biereg spoke sharply, sounding just like my mother.

My face felt hot. I blotted my watery eyes with my stiff white napkin. Without thinking, I stood and stumbled away from the table, leaving my food all scrambled together, uneaten.

"Edith," I heard Julius call. "Edith, wait . . . wait."

But I didn't turn around. I ran to our empty cabin and threw myself onto my berth, covering my head with my pillow to muffle my loud sobs.

After that I avoided Frau Biereg. When she said I ate like a bird, I was sure she knew how I'd stuffed myself with ice cream. She was right to scold me, just as Mutti would have.

But my shame didn't change my eating habits. The next day, I was back at the ice cream counter five times. I knew I shouldn't, and I felt embarrassed when the steward rolled his eyes each time I asked for another serving.

Still, I couldn't stop myself. There was nothing else I wanted to eat. I was starving; the smooth, sweet, frozen milk was my only comfort.

I'd do anything to fill the hole.

Most days, those of us who weren't sick spent time sitting together on the upper deck, gazing out at the endless ocean. Some days, when the sea was calm, I sat for hours in the early morning, bundled in a beige wool blanket with the word "*Deutschland*" sewn on it in black thread. I could hardly feel the ship move. The heavy smell of salt hung in the air. I could taste it on my lips.

Several evenings, though, the seas were rough. One evening, I decided to write Mina my first letter, but the ship rocked so hard that my pen jumped all over the paper in childlike scribbles. Gertie laughed as she watched me try to make the words "*Liebe* Mina" legible.

At times, we were barely able to stand upright anywhere on board. Then, some passengers would lean over the ship's rails, losing whatever was in their stomachs. We called it "feeding the fish." The champion feeder was Liesel, who was so sick through the whole trip that we hardly saw her.

On the rough nights, the ship's sharp, jerking swings would send us into our berths, forcing us to climb into bed. There was nothing else to do, nowhere we could be safe.

When the seas were calmer, Gertie and I would watch the evening sky's show of brilliant purples, oranges, and blues. We'd talk about all sorts of things.

"I wonder what will become of my cats, Theodor and Heinrich," I said to Gertie one quiet, dark night. "Heinrich is black with white feet and Theodor has orange and white stripes."

"Your pets?"

"Sort of. My parents don't . . . didn't allow me to keep cats as pets. They didn't want me to feed them. We live above my father's store. Everyone in town used to come in to buy feed for their animals, but we had trouble with the mice that got into the burlap sacks. So my parents took in cats to eat the mice. But I loved those cats and I would sneak out and feed them whenever I could. I named them, too."

Passing the hours in deck chairs, we would tell each other imaginary stories about the passengers strolling by: where they came from, where they were going, whom they had left behind. While we talked, we always kept an eye on the water, hoping to catch sight of a flying fish flipping up alongside the ship. When we saw one, we would jump up to get a closer look. I decided that they were lucky—even magical. I was sure that each one I saw improved my chances of seeing my parents again.

Once, while looking for fish, we saw a dot off in the distance. As it grew larger and larger, we realized that it was another ship. Eventually we could read the name on its side: *Europa*. Closer and closer, then finally turning a little to the right and away, the *Europa* passed us, blowing its horn in greeting while passengers yelled "Hallo!" from both decks.

This was strangely disturbing to me. As I looked at the passengers on the deck of the *Europa*, I realized that it had been days since I had seen a new face, anyone who wasn't on our ship. Small and safe, the *Deutschland* had become my own little world.

One night Gertie confessed to me that she liked Peter. A few nights passed before I told her I had a secret, too.

"Promise not to tell anyone?" I said, as the sunset's colors grew deeper.

"Yes."

"You sure?"

"Of course." She rolled her brown eyes at me, an expression that only Gertie could make. "Tell me. I told you my secret."

I shifted uncomfortably in my deck chair.

"I tell you everything," she insisted. "You're my best friend now."

When she said that, I was surprised. We had only known each other for four days. But then I realized that I didn't have a best friend back in Stockstadt. I didn't have *any* friends—only Mina, and now she was gone.

So I figured Gertie was right. She was my best friend now. I turned to face her, hoping she wouldn't laugh.

"I . . . I kind of like someone, too," I confessed.

"Who? Who? Who do you *kiiiind of* like?"

Before I could answer, she smiled. "I know who."

We said it together, at the same time: "Julius."

I liked so many things about him—his wavy brown hair, his height, his deep blue eyes. The funny things he did to make me laugh, and how he winked at me sometimes, as if we had a secret. I thought about Julius more than anyone—except my parents.

But no matter what I was doing, even when I was laughing with Julius, a part of me remained in Stockstadt.

I was living in two worlds at once. Every few hours, I checked the ship's clock in the dining hall, counted backward to the time in Germany, and figured out exactly what I would have been doing if I had been at home. I might have been playing table tennis or shuffleboard or tag on the *Deutschland*—but in my mind, I was looking around the side of the house for Theodor and Heinrich, collecting the eggs from the chickens, or riding on the back of Mina's red bicycle. Any game, any time, I was here . . . and there.

On the nights Julius, Peter, Gertie, and I played bingo with a dozen other passengers in the dining hall, I didn't check the clock quite as often. I liked sitting next to Julius, who always seemed to have the winning card.

"Look," I said when I noticed he needed one more number to win. Then we would all crowd around him. "Julius almost has bingo."

"What can I say, E-Edit?" Julius smiled, using his pet name for me. He looked over at our nearly empty cards, shrugged his shoulders, and said, "I'm just lucky."

He *was* lucky. He came from the beautiful city of Cologne. For him, this journey was an adventure, not a loss. He had his parents. His family was together. That was one reason I liked him; he seemed to have everything.

"BINGO!" Julius shouted as the announcer called out another number. And I felt as if I had won, too, just by sitting next to him.

————

Two nights before we arrived in New York, the crew threw a special party for all the passengers. We stood along the ballroom walls and watched.

At the dance there was a colored man—the first Negro I had ever seen; before this, the only colored people I had ever heard of in Germany were in a traveling circus, and of course we had never seen a traveling circus in Stockstadt. Later I learned that he was an American doctor who had taken a medical internship in Vienna and was on his way back to Atlanta, Georgia, wherever that was.

As the music played, he approached Gertie. "May I have this dance?" he said in German, bowing slightly before her.

"I don't know," said Gertie. "I don't feel too good."

"Yes." He laughed. "You look a little green. So maybe dancing would make you feel better?" He extended his hand to Gertie.

After the song was over, we gathered around Gertie, who looked a little dazed, but pleased. The man, who was a graceful dancer, made it look easy to keep time and do the right steps. He asked whether any of us had ever heard of the Lambeth Walk.

"It came from the musical *Me and My Girl*," he said, starting to show us the first steps of the dance. Then he held up a hand, excused himself, and went over to the bandleader to request "The Lambeth Walk." As they played the first few bars, he strutted back to us in a funny walking style, with his feet stepping far out ahead of his body and his elbows sticking out at his sides. In the show, the man said, several couples lined up and performed the same steps together, almost like a chorus line in a movie.

I, Gertie, Peter, Julius, Franzi, and even Liesel clapped, hopped, tapped our feet, and stepped high, imitating the man's grace and style. Other passengers—including a few adults—joined in our chorus line. For at least an hour, we shook and kicked, counting out steps, laughing and sweating.

*Eins, zwei, drei, vier.* "One, two, three, four." For the first time in longer than I could remember, I forgot about home. I wasn't thinking about whether my parents would get to America, whether I would ever see Mina again, whether she would remember to feed Theodor and Heinrich. I didn't even look at the clock.

But I froze when I noticed one of the Nazi stewards watching our every move. His arms were folded across his chest, and his eyes were narrow, as if he were recording who was there and what we were doing. I elbowed Gertie, calling her attention to him. She looked at him, then waved her hand as if to say, "Don't worry."

It was clear from the steward's rigid expression that he didn't approve of the dance. But he didn't stop us. His scowl reminded me of a poster I had seen just a few months earlier, in front of the music hall in the next town. The colors in the poster had caught my eye, and I had grabbed Vati's elbow to get him to stop walking and look at it with me.

The poster pictured a cartoon of a colored man, wearing a fancy tuxedo but with the face of a monkey, playing the saxophone in a musical performance. On the lapel of his tuxedo was a Jewish star. Written in bright white letters that popped out against the red background were two words: *Entartete Musik*—"degenerate music."

"What does this mean, Vati?" I pointed to the two bold words.

"That's what the Nazis call jazz. They are trying to ban it and other new music. They call that music degenerate, Bolshevik, or Jewish, even though it has nothing to do with us."

The Nazis would have called the Lambeth Walk and our dancing degenerate, too, I thought. But at that moment, I didn't care. I couldn't wait to show Betty how to do the Lambeth Walk. She had always introduced me to things. Here, I thought, was my chance to show her something new. I memorized the steps carefully—for the two of us.

The next morning, as Gertie and I went to breakfast, we hooked our arms and high-stepped into the dining hall, bumping into Peter and Julius, who linked arms with us and began to wiggle, too, laughing and dancing as we sat down at a table.

Then a thin-lipped woman dressed in a white blouse

and crisp navy jacket and skirt approached us. She stood silent as, one by one, we stopped dancing.

"You're going to America," she finally said in slow, careful German with an American accent. "You're going to live there. I watched you dancing with that man last night."

She looked from one of us to the next. We all shifted uncomfortably in our chairs. Finally she spoke again.

"You should know," she said, "we don't do that in America."

Gertie and I exchanged a look of panic. Was America like Germany? Could someone call you degenerate and tell everyone else to have nothing to do with you?

I knew that America had a quota for Jews, allowing only a small number to enter the country every year. This meant that Americans probably didn't like Jews much, but it had never occurred to me that Americans might be as hateful as the Nazis.

Surely my parents wouldn't send me to a country like that. Surely things must be better in America.

I had never questioned this idea—but now, I didn't know. When that woman said, "We don't do that in America," I wondered what they *did* do.

## 5

## THIS IS "GOODBYE"

I see the beam towers!" Peter was yelling, pounding on our cabin door, though everyone inside was sound asleep. "I see the beam towers!"

It was still dark when I opened my eyes. At first, as I struggled to wake up, I thought I was in my bed at home, listening to the roaring woodstove in the living room. But when I looked around me—around the ship's cabin— nothing was familiar.

Then the ocean's waves jolted the *Deutschland*, water slamming hard on the side of the ship so that a heavy spray splashed against our little porthole. I looked over to Gertie's berth and saw that she was rubbing her eyes. Her familiar face was a comfort.

"Beam towers?" I asked Gertie. "What are beam towers?"

"Hurry up, Edith!" Gertie tossed off her duvet. "Let's go."

"Where are you going?" Franzi said, barely awake. "It's freezing out there."

"We'll be fine," Gertie said as she threw on her red sweater, the orange still in her pocket. As we ran up the spiral staircase to the upper deck, a brisk wind slapped us. Maybe Franzi was right, I thought, shivering in the chilly darkness.

"Look!" Peter pointed off into the distance toward a faint light, barely visible on the dark horizon. "That's the Statue of Liberty. Julius and I have been out here looking for it since three-thirty this morning. I saw it first!"

"I don't think so," Gertie said, pulling her red sweater tighter around herself.

"Yes, I did," said Peter. "I saw it first, didn't I, Julius?"

Julius didn't answer him; in fact, he didn't take his eyes off the horizon. "You don't believe me?" Peter pressed Gertie.

"I don't believe you because I don't see a thing."

"Maybe you should keep watching," I said, agreeing with Gertie. "We're going back to bed." It was too cold to stay on deck.

"No, wait," he said. "You have to look real closely. See that white speck . . ."

Gertie squinted. "Wake us when you can see the lady,"

she said, grasping my arm and guiding me back to the staircase. "C'mon, Edith. I'm *freezing*."

It wasn't even an hour before Peter was back, pounding on the cabin door again. "Gertie, Edith, get up! Now! Hurry up! Now you can almost talk to the lady!"

But not quite, we discovered when we went back on the deck. I could barely make out her shape in the spotlights that Peter called beam towers. Still, my heart began to pound.

"This is my first look at my new country," Julius said, narrowing his eyes and staring at the light.

"Your country?" I was confused. "But what about Germany?"

"Germany *was* my country," he said.

"*Was* your country?" I asked. As much as I liked Julius, sometimes I just didn't understand him.

"Yes, was," he said, never turning to look at me. "America *is* my country now."

This idea instantly divided us. How could he suddenly be an American when he hadn't even set foot on her soil yet? We were all angry at Germany over what had happened to us. Still, it was our *Heimat*. That one word describes the people, the Kühkopf and the Rhein River, the food, the music, even the beer (though we were too young to have tasted more than a few sips of it)—all we knew as home. Germany was still my country. Abandoning it would be like disowning my own family.

But Julius's family was here with him. Maybe he could separate his family from Germany, but I couldn't—and wouldn't.

I kept my eye on the distant, steadily growing white spot. What would it be like to finally get off the ship? Suddenly, I couldn't stand the thought of parting from Julius, Peter, and Gertie . . . especially Gertie. Her round, freckly face had become as familiar to me as Mina's. I had watched Gertie closely the entire journey, and I had learned some of the little things that made her unique: the way she chewed her food slowly to get the most out of each bite, the way she bit her finger when she wasn't sure of what she thought, the way her eyes became almond-shaped just before she laughed.

When I told Franzi that I was sad about leaving the ship and saying goodbye to my friends, she said that we would have a few more days together in New York. Knowing that was a relief, but now I had a new worry. When we had left Germany, I counted the hours away from home. Now, as we approached New York, I was counting the hours until I would have to leave Gertie.

As the sky lightened, the statue grew before our eyes, and now Gertie couldn't wait to show it to the little boy who had wanted to go to the zoo. She wanted him to know that she had told him the truth: this journey would take him to America. She knew exactly where to find him. Each morning, he would leave the cabin at dawn and curl up in his usual spot near the spiral staircase.

"See? See?" She walked behind him, holding him by the shoulders and directing his attention through the ship's railings. "I told you you'd see the Statue of Liberty."

Then she awkwardly lifted him so that he could peer over the railing. Gertie wasn't that big or strong, so she couldn't hold up a five-year-old boy for long. He didn't help her by wedging his feet up in the railing. In fact, he barely moved.

"There, now you see," she said.

The boy stared. It seemed that he was looking, but not seeing. His deadened eyes scared me.

"Isn't that something?" Gertie asked him.

The warm morning light bathed the face of the Statue of Liberty, and just as we passed in front of it, the skyline of New York appeared. We lined the railings, stunned into silence.

Some of the grownups began to cry, falling to their knees on the deck, collapsing like the parents we'd left on the dock back in Bremen. That scared me. But then I realized that they were weeping tears of joy. "America, America!" they chanted, like the name of a long-lost love.

"Isn't it spectacular?" Gertie whispered into the boy's ear.

Still, there was no answer. It was as if he couldn't see or speak, as if he were a broken toy that couldn't move anymore.

———

I don't remember much about Ellis Island: lots of luggage, long lines, and health inspections. I do remember that after hours of waiting, a woman much younger than my mother, with dark brown bobbed hair and ruby-red fingernails, came up to us, and, with a warm smile, introduced herself. She immediately took three of the children, including the broken boy, to a private room where we saw some adults waiting. I suppose they went to be with relatives in New York; I never saw them again.

When the lady returned, I couldn't take my eyes off her. She looked like a doll. I had never before seen a woman with painted fingernails. She wore lipstick and eye shadow, too. In Germany under Hitler, nail polish and makeup were considered sinful.

I couldn't take my eyes off her necklace either—a shiny silver Star of David. At first, when I noticed it, I cringed, afraid that someone might attack her. But she didn't seem to be scared at all. The star wasn't hidden under her blouse. Its silver flashed in the light. Maybe America would be different from Germany after all.

"Isn't she beautiful?" I whispered to Gertie, while we waited in line.

"Yes," she said, as enchanted as I was by the lady's appearance. "She looks like the mannequin in the *Deutschland*'s shop window. Only she's real."

I struggled to remember some of the English I had learned back home from the German Jewish weekly newspaper. My father and I did the lessons that the paper featured, but I had never before exchanged an English word with someone who actually spoke the language. I had the idea that the word "goodbye" was an all-purpose greeting, for both coming and going. The only other two things I was sure I understood were "fine" and "How do you do?"

So when the beautiful American woman spoke to me—explaining, I think, that she was a kind of host who would show us around New York—I was eager to impress her with my English and begin a relationship with the first American I had ever met.

"Goodbye," I said confidently. "How do you do?" I smiled, showing off the few words I knew.

"What?" the lady asked, the crease in her brow deepening.

"Goodbye," I said again, sure of my English. And then when she didn't seem to understand what I was saying, I quickly added in German, *"Guten Tag?"*

"I think you mean 'hello.' " She spoke so fast I couldn't follow what she was saying. Then she said more slowly, "Heellllooo."

"Hallo?"

"Yes." She smiled, then giggled, "Hello." Was she laughing at me?

"This is 'goodbye,' " she said, waving with her hand back and forth, with the same gesture I had used to wave goodbye to my parents. It was the gesture that Julius had corrected when I first met him, warning me that the wave could be seen as a "heil Hitler."

I burst into tears. Even if I didn't know the right gesture and words in English, I was very familiar with "goodbye."


Soon I had to deal with another goodbye. An hour or so later, Julius was about to leave for Grand Central Terminal, where he and his family were to board a train that went directly to Chicago. The five of us—Julius, Peter, Gertie, Liesel, and I—awkwardly eyed one another, not knowing what to say or what to do. We stood in a circle in the huge main building on Ellis Island, uncomfortably waiting for someone to say something. I squinted up at the sun's blinding rays, angling through the huge arched windows of the old building. Hard to believe that only hours earlier, as we approached the harbor, the same sun's soft rays had welcomed us with a pink glow on the Statue of Liberty.

Finally, Julius moved, reaching toward Peter, and then Peter toward Liesel, Gertie, and me. We huddled together, arms knotted around each other like a woven basket. I remember thinking that the five of us looked like we formed a human lifeboat . . . and, in a way, we had.

Julius asked each of us to write, warning Gertie if she didn't, "I'll come after you in *Zay*-attle," as she called it.

Then he turned to me.

"Of course, I don't expect *you* to write," he said. "Maybe we'll be in the same school. After all, we'll both be living in Chicago."

"Y—yeees," I said, my voice squeaking as I tried to speak around that lump in my throat. "I . . . I'm sure we'll see each other all the time."

"I'll figure out where your aunt and uncle live. Their last name is Westerfeld—same as yours, right?"

"Right."

"I'll find them somehow," Julius promised, giving me a quick, clumsy hug and running toward his waiting family. He called out, "Bye, E-Edit!" I smiled and then bit my lip so I wouldn't cry, watching him as he walked out the door.

"I'll find you, one way or another!" he called back to me before the door slammed. I tried to see him through the window, but I couldn't. He was lost in the crowd.

"One way or another," I whispered, "one way or another."

The three days in New York were so busy that we didn't have time to think about anything. I suppose the tour guides planned it that way. We saw the city's great tourist attractions: the Empire State Building, the Rockettes at Radio City Music Hall, the Chrysler Building, the Whitney Museum of American Art, Rockefeller Plaza, and Macy's department store.

What an adventure it was for Gertie and me to be in

bustling New York City! We were from sleepy little villages in Germany. Stockstadt was a long, long way from here—a world away. I couldn't think of how I could describe the city to my parents and Mina. They wouldn't be able to imagine these skyscrapers that were a whole city in one building. They looked like man-made mountains. Betty had written in one of her first postcards home that she had a stiff neck from standing on the sidewalk and trying to see the top of the Empire State Building. Now I could see why.

"*Wow,*" I said as Gertie and I looked up at the face of the skyscrapers. "*Wow.*"

"*Wow,*" Gertie echoed. We couldn't see the top; it ended in the clouds. I felt even smaller than I was. "I'm dizzy."

"Yeah, it feels like we've been spinning in circles."

"I feel like I'm still on the boat," Gertie said, trying to regain her balance.

"Don't feed the fish," I told her, and we both laughed.

Macy's department store, which took up a whole city block, made the *Deutschland*'s clothing shop look like a stylish American's closet, and a rather small one at that. At Macy's, dozens of mannequins modeled the latest fashions in sophisticated poses—smoking a cigarette in a slender silver cigarette holder, carrying beaded white gloves or a monkey-fur hand muff, peering out dramatically from a veiled dark hat. Gertie and I tried to pose like each of the mannequins.

We stayed at the George Washington Hotel for two

nights. When I crawled into bed each night, I felt seasick.

"Gertie," I whispered, so I wouldn't wake Franzi and Liesel, who were sharing the other double bed. "I can't sleep."

"Why not?" She hadn't fallen asleep yet either.

"Don't you feel it? The rocking . . . like you're still on the boat?"

"Oh, is that what that is?" she whispered. "I thought I was just dizzy."

"What if it never stops?" I asked, forgetting to keep my voice down. "What if we never really feel like we are off the boat?"

"*Mädchen, beruhigt euch.* Quiet down, girls," Franzi said before Gertie could answer. "I'm trying to get some sleep."

Each morning we woke up excited about whatever was on our schedule for that day. New York was a whirlwind of things new to me: Escalators. Elevators. Subway rides. Pull-down window shades. Soda fountains. Kellogg's Rice Krispies. Peanut butter. Grapefruit. Bubblegum. Milkshakes. There were all kinds of people, too—dark-skinned, light-skinned, some speaking languages that I *knew* weren't English.

One evening, the guides took us on a tour of the city on a double-decker bus—another first for me. Its upper level was open and the March air was cold and raw, but we four remaining friends—Peter, Liesel, Gertie, and me—

squeezed together to stay warm while we took in the views of the skyline as the bus drove along the Hudson River. Across the river, we were told, was "another state," which translated literally meant "another country." In the other direction, the city against the night sky looked like jewels on black velvet.

But beneath each happy adventure in New York, every conversation, every joke I shared with Gertie, was the nagging awareness that soon we would separate. Sometimes I would count the hours. I comforted myself on the second day with the idea that I had a whole thirty-six more hours with her. But then it was down to thirty-three, twenty-nine, twenty-seven . . .

The next day, we boarded the subway headed toward Rockefeller Center, to see the Disney cartoon *Snow White and the Seven Dwarfs* at Radio City Music Hall. A man carrying a small boy, about five years old, stepped onto the train with us, followed a few feet behind by a young woman. Just as she was about to step onto the train, the doors slammed shut, leaving her on the platform alone. The man motioned to her through the window, telling her to meet them at the next station. But the boy didn't understand. As the train pulled away, separating the boy from the woman, he let out an agonizing shriek: *"Mommm-mmmy!"*

We were stunned. None of us in the group could take our eyes off the boy.

*"Mommmmmmyyy!"* The boy could not be comforted. The man picked up his son and spoke gently to him in his ear. But he kept sobbing in deep gasps.

In our group, nobody said a word. I could not stand to watch, and I could not look away. I didn't want to see the boy's face; instead I watched his small foot, in a scuffed brown shoe, hanging loosely around his father's hip. Each time the boy screamed for his mother, his foot would become rigid.

*"Mommmmmmyyyy,"* the boy screamed again, as the train rushed toward the next station. He was gasping for breath, his face bright red. I worried that he might turn blue if he couldn't get enough air. Tears soaked the collar of his shirt and the shoulder of his father's gray overcoat.

Peter kept watching, but he leaned against the pole to keep his balance while he covered his ears so he wouldn't have to hear the shrieks. Liesel dabbed at the corners of her eyes with the sleeve of her jacket. Gertie grabbed my arm and squeezed so hard that I had to tell her to loosen her grip.

"Sorry," she said, as I tried to draw a deep breath. As the train slowed, Gertie took my hand and whispered, "He reminds me of that boy who wanted to go to the zoo."

He reminded me of all of us.

*Snow White and the Seven Dwarfs* was a brand-new film, just released. The group leaders probably thought it would be thrilling to see a new movie in a grand New York movie house. But to us, it was frightening. Gertie and I dug our fingernails into each other's arms during the really scary parts, and, after the movie was over, we tried to figure out what it was about. We weren't really sure, but we agreed that we didn't ever want to see it again. When I admitted to Gertie that I was afraid that I was going to have nightmares about it, Gertie started singing the tune to "Whistle While You Work," a song from one of the happier parts of the movie. For the next day, whenever one of us would get sad or scared, we would sing that tune.

But no one sang on the day we had to say goodbye. At Grand Central Terminal, Peter was boarding a train to a place none of us had ever heard of: Alabama. All we knew was that it was in the South. Liesel was going to a nearby state that none of us could remember how to say—Massachusetts. Gertie was headed clear across the continent to *Zay*-attle, Washington. "The train ride there is half as long as our journey across the ocean," she said. "I could be nearly home again."

Franzi was at the station, too, to see us off. Then she would board another ship to return to Germany, she said, where she hoped to escort more children to America. She told us that she would keep up with "all my children," as if we belonged to her, promising to write once a month and to send us pictures from our days on the *Deutschland* and in New York.

I was taking the *20th Century Limited* to Chicago, but it didn't really matter to me where I was going; all I knew was that I had to say goodbye again. I felt sick, just as I had when I was waving to my parents, waiting for the ship to leave.

When Liesel, who was the first to go, was about to board her train, we stood together on the platform, exchanging hugs, checking to see that we had the pieces of paper on which she had written her address. She climbed the steps into the train and took a window seat so we could watch her as the train pulled away. She pressed her hands and nose against the window. But before long, steam puffed up off the track as the train slowly began to move, the way it had in Stockstadt.

Only two weeks earlier, I had looked out a train window, too. Now it felt like a long time ago. I wasn't sure Liesel could see me, but I found myself waving wildly to her, just as I did on the boat when I said goodbye to my parents. Then I caught myself, and changed the motion to a gentle flick of my fingers, fearing that there were secret Nazis watching us.

We returned to the hard, wooden benches in the station to wait half an hour until Peter's train left. While we sat, he banged his luggage handle back and forth. Franzi asked him to stop. "It's irritating," she said, sounding impatient for the first time.

Peter, who never knew quite what to do, wouldn't

look any of us in the eye to say goodbye. Though he was older than Gertie, Julius, and me, sometimes he acted much younger. He tried not to make too much of leaving, behaving as if he would be pounding on our cabin door tomorrow morning, ready for another game of tag or hide-and-seek. "Next time we play, I'll beat you," he kept saying, as if he'd see us tomorrow. "You'll see."

And me—I felt sick. I was being ripped away. They were making me leave again. My friends on the ship weren't my real family, not my sister or Mina, but I knew them and they knew me. I'd gotten used to being with them. We had seen each other through this long journey. Now I was going to people I didn't know, who didn't know anything about me, who might not even speak my language.

As she was about to board her train, Gertie stared at me, hard—the way I had looked at Vati as we sat on the train to Bremen. We were both memorizing a face we couldn't bear to forget.

It hurt me to see what she was doing. She must have known, because she stopped staring and tried to comfort me by saying, "*Es ist in Ordnung*. It'll be okay."

If only I could stay with Gertie, I thought, *then* I would be okay. We would support each other, putting our heads together and figuring out this strange new world.

"Give me your address," she said. In my bag, I found a piece of paper and the pen Vati had given me just before I left. I knew my Chicago address by heart, and I wrote it on the paper. I'd memorized the numbers and words on the boat; it was the only thing anchoring me to a future.

"I'll write you," she said when she saw my tears. "I promise." Then she added, "I have something for you."

Gertie pulled out an extra passport picture that had been folded into the pouch that hung around her neck behind her number, 253. Then she took my pen, scribbled something on the back of the picture, and handed the picture and pen to me.

I stared at the picture, which had been taken only a few weeks earlier. Gertie appeared so young in the photograph, with her apple cheeks and freckles. Now, she looked different, older.

I turned over the photo and looked at what she had written: *21 März 1938. Zur Erinnerung. Deine Freundin, Gertie Katz.* "March 21, 1938. For remembrance. Your friend, Gertie Katz."

## 6

## WILLKOMMEN IN AMERIKA

It was just a torn scrap of paper, the bottom half of a billing statement that Vati used to send to his customers when he still had business. "Don't lose this, Tiddy," my father had said as he scribbled something on the half page and handed it to me just before we left for the ship.

I looked at what he had written; it appeared to be a street location, but the words and numbers were out of order.

Vati saw that I was confused: "This is where you're going. It's Onkel Jakob's address."

On the ship—every day, sometimes twice a day—I had checked to make sure the paper was still in the inside pocket of the suitcase. I had memorized the address, but would I mix up the numbers or forget the name of the street? Maybe I wouldn't be able to pronounce the words in English. Then what would I do?

Each day, as I handled the paper, the edges became more ragged and the blue ink faded. But I figured that as long as the writing was still legible, someone could read it. Someone would point me in the right direction to 927 East 76th Street, Chicago, Illinois, U.S.A. The smudged scrap of paper was my compass.

Now I clasped it tightly in my left hand, lugging my heavy suitcase in my right, as I shuffled through Grand Central Terminal's enormous waiting room. Franzi had bought my train ticket and was helping me find the platform where I would board the *20th Century Limited*, a fast, modern train that would carry me from New York City to Chicago in only sixteen hours.

Franzi held out my ticket and some American money. I clutched all this with my scrap of paper as she pointed at a doorway. Just beyond, I could see the tracks where huge, noisy trains stood steaming.

"I'll come visit you in Chicago one day," she called after me, waving as I headed toward the archway.

"I'd like that," I said, even though I knew she couldn't hear me. By now I was more numb than sad. Franzi was the last person from the ship I had to say goodbye to.

As I slowly walked behind a crowd of people down the long red carpet leading to the train's cars, I looked closely at the strange money in my hand. I was so used to brownish pink Reichsmarks that, to me, these green American dollars looked fake. I couldn't believe they were worth anything. But everything here seemed inside out, so anything was possible.

Maybe Franzi had just made me rich, I thought. Maybe this money could pay for my family's passage to America. Then I recalled what she had said: "Here, you can buy yourself a drink and some supper on the train." That couldn't amount to much.

I had expected that I wouldn't understand the language, but not knowing the money was a whole new worry. For all the ways he had tried to prepare me, Vati hadn't said anything to me about American money. What else hadn't he thought of?

"Good afternoon, young lady," said a tall colored man, smiling as he took my suitcase and held out his hand to help me up the four narrow stairs into the car. He was wearing a crisp, gray-and-white uniform. Two of his front teeth were capped with shiny silver.

As I made my way down the aisle, I noticed that all the other passengers were adults, mostly men wearing well-cut, sharply pressed business suits. The few women on the train seemed to be traveling with them. Had their fancy dresses and fashionable business suits come from Macy's? One lady who had already taken her seat was wearing a copper-colored jacket, just like the one Gertie had pointed to in the window of the ship's clothing shop.

"Gertie, look at that!" I said out loud as I turned around to point out the lady's jacket to her, only to realize Gertie wasn't with me anymore.

I felt awkward and out of place in my handmade skirt, smocked blouse, and sturdy, old-fashioned brown shoes. With my 108 tag hanging from my neck, I must have looked like a parcel. Nobody had told me whether I should keep it on, so I thought I'd better leave it, just to be safe. Besides, I figured the other kids were still wearing their tags, too.

The other passengers watched me walk down the aisle. I felt sure they were whispering about me to their traveling companions.

I found a window seat and settled into its soft gray cushion, my feet dangling just above the floor. The train jerked forward and pulled away from the station. Gazing out the window, I watched passing scenes in the backyards of redbrick buildings. Several times I saw boys about my age playing a game with a stick and a ball, yelling and running whenever they hit the ball.

Even though it was cold outside, clotheslines were strung from metal stairways attached to every apartment window. They were weighted down with garments of all sizes, flapping in the wind. From some open windows, mothers leaned out, calling to their children.

Behind the houses, the sun was setting in stripes of

orange and purple. It was the only thing that looked familiar to me. I had never felt so alone. I wanted to tell someone—anyone—"*Ich hab' Angst*. I'm scared." But even if I said it, who would understand?

After we had traveled an hour or so, the man with the shiny teeth came down the aisle. "Coffee, tea," he said, pointing toward the next car, which I realized must be the dining car. He looked at me. I didn't want to pass all those well-dressed adults again, but I was hungry, so I made myself stand and walk all the way to the dining car, where several colored porters were serving coffee, tea, milk, and cookies. The man with the capped-tooth smile stopped by my table and offered me extra cookies. I wished I knew enough English to talk to him. He looked at me with kind, dark eyes but didn't speak. Maybe he knew I couldn't understand.

When I returned to my seat, the train's gentle rocking lulled me into a strange half sleep. I never got up for dinner. Several times during the night I heard the train's whistle, but it didn't really wake me. I wasn't sure if I was asleep or awake but I knew that I wasn't at home and I wasn't on the *Deutschland*.

It was barely light outside when an announcement crackled over the train's loudspeaker. The only word I understood was "Indiana," which I remembered from the maps Vati and I had studied. I opened my eyes to flat, brown fields. They looked strange and ugly, nothing like the grand mountains I loved in Germany. It had never crossed my mind that mountains weren't everywhere in the world. Of course, I had seen pictures in books of different landscapes, but they were just pictures, like a fairy tale. Now, here in Indiana, the land stretched out as far as I could see without so much as a tree.

As I looked out the window and saw my reflection in the glass, I thought about my sister. Over the past year, I had started to look more like the pictures my parents had taken of Betty just before she left. I smiled to think that with each mile, I was getting closer and closer to her. I wondered if Betty was on her way to the train station to meet me. Thinking of seeing my sister, I could hardly sit still. I couldn't wait to teach her the Lambeth Walk. I couldn't wait to hug her tightly—something we never did in Germany. I wouldn't want to let her go ever again. I didn't want to spend another birthday without her and I had another one to celebrate in just a couple of months.

I wondered who would come to welcome me. I didn't know anyone else in Chicago, but I expected that what family I had—Betty, Onkel Jakob, Aunt Mildred, and my cousin Dorothy—would be at the station to greet me.

Restless and bored, I decided to pass the time by going to the dining car for breakfast. I hadn't eaten anything since yesterday's cookies, but I was so excited that I didn't have much appetite now. I didn't even know how to ask for breakfast, but I noticed that other passengers were reading menus and speaking to the porters, who soon brought heavy trays. Each tray held different food: eggs and meat, oatmeal, toast, fruit, coffee, tea. I hoped I could just point to something on the menu and give the man with the capped-tooth grin all my money. But when I sat down by the window, the man said, "Good morning," and handed me a plate with two pieces of toast, strawberry jelly, and tea. I held out my money, but he shook his head no and walked away.

My eyes were glued to the window as I ate most of one piece of toast, watching the landscape outside the window change from farmland to buildings. The train slowed down as it passed small houses or big brick buildings that lined one street after another. All the buildings looked clean and neat, but there were so many of them, crowded so close together. Was this Chicago?

As we traveled deeper into the city, I saw fewer brick buildings; instead there were old shabby wooden shops mixed in with tall stone buildings. The train slowed down. Outside, crowds of people crept along the sidewalk, together forming what looked like a huge caterpillar. Some buildings were as tall as the ones I had seen in New York. As we entered the station and screeched to a stop, passengers gathered their things, stood up, and began moving down the aisles. I stood up, too, and made my way to the door.

"Miss," the silver-toothed porter said to me, offering his hand—just as he did for all the ladies—as I was about to step off the train. He smiled at me again and said something in English. His face was so friendly that I knew he must be welcoming me to Chicago.

I smiled back. *"Schönen Dank,"* I said politely, forgetting where I was for a moment.

As I stepped into the cold, I saw several men unloading trunks and bags onto the platform. Tiny snowflakes dotted the gray air. It usually didn't snow in Stockstadt this late in March, so we hadn't packed my heavy winter coat—we knew I would outgrow it by next year. Shivering, I tried to close the collar of my gray wool coat, but somewhere along the way, I had lost the button.

"Edith?" A tall man approached me as I watched the porter unload my brown suitcase. It was easy to spot because it was the only one with a large black, red, and white *Deutschland* baggage sticker slapped on its side.

"Are you Edith?" He pronounced my name with a "th," the English way.

I looked up, startled to see that this man resembled my father. He was a little older, but he had the same sharp nose, gray hair, receding hairline—all just like Vati. Even his little round glasses were the same.

*"Guten Tag!"* He extended a large, familiar hand to shake mine.

"Onkel Jakob?" I said as my whole body began to shiver. I was sure this man could feel the tremors as he shook my hand.

"Call me Uncle Jack," he said in English, and then repeating in German, *"Sag' Uncle Jack zu mir."*

In my mind, aboard the ship and on the train, I had played out this scene dozens of times. I had wished and waited to hear those words. "Call me Uncle Jack. Uncle Jack *zu mir.*" I hoped they would be in German, but in any language, they meant one thing: I had made it.

No need to keep my scrap of paper anymore. No need to worry about what I would do if I got lost. No need to wonder how I would talk to Uncle Jack. Lucky for me, he still knew German. A spark deep within me lit up my face with a broad smile.

*"Es gibt eine Familienähnlichkeit.* There is a family resemblance," he said, returning my smile. "You look like your father as a little boy."

Of course, I wouldn't have known, but it was wonderful to be with someone who did.

*"Und du siehst aus wie er jetzt als Mann aussieht.* And you look like him as a man," I answered. Uncle Jack laughed, and I noticed that his eyes were shining the way my father's used to, the way he looked before the neighbors taunted him and beat him in the stairwell.

I looked around for the other members of my family. "It's just me," Uncle Jack said quietly.

"*Wo ist meine Schwester?* Where is my sister?" I asked.

"She couldn't come."

When he said that, I could feel my face fall.

"Aunt Mildred?"

"No, she's not here either," Uncle Jack answered, still speaking German. "There were some things she had to do. But you'll meet her at the apartment."

Staring up at Uncle Jack, I saw he was staring at me, too.

"You can take that off now," he said in English, pointing to my number. I eyed him again, stunned by how much he had the same squinty brown eyes framed in a net of tiny wrinkles, the same crooked smile, even the same high forehead as my father. He looked so familiar, yet so foreign.

"Go on now, take it off," he continued in English, motioning to me to take the tag from my neck.

Now I understood what he meant. I looked down at my number, 108. I had gotten used to wearing it; I wasn't sure I wanted to give it up. I didn't know how to answer him in English. Instead, I held tightly to the tag, shaking my head. I wasn't ready to let go of the one thing that tied me to my friends on the ship.

"Welcome to America." Uncle Jack spread his arms

wide, palms up. He smiled broadly, as if to show me this new world where I wouldn't need to wear a tag.

The only word I understood was "America." I stared up at him blankly.

He said it again, a little slower, arms even wider this time.

Still, I gripped my 108 tag. Finally, he gave in, speaking German so I would understand. *Willkommen in Amerika.*

## YOU BATHE ON TUESDAYS AND THURSDAYS

The smell of mothballs flooded the dark hallway as Uncle Jack pushed open the heavy wooden door of the apartment that would now be my home.

"Mother," Uncle Jack called out in English as he stepped inside. I knew that word, and I was confused. His mother is Oma Sarah, I thought. She couldn't possibly be here; I had left her in Germany two weeks ago.

"Mother!" Uncle Jack called again, louder this time, dropping his keys on a small table, under a lamp with a fringed shade.

"All right, I'm coming!" It was a woman's voice, yelling in English from another room. Still, no one appeared. I let my suitcase down onto the floor as I hung behind Uncle Jack, waiting and wondering what "Mother" could be doing.

At last—faintly, then louder—I heard a *thump-thump-*

*thump*. With each thump, the fringe on the lamp shade shook.

Finally, a tall, bulky woman walked into the room, her face mostly hidden by eyeglasses and a mass of curly gray hair. She wore a stretched-out beige sweater, a faded black skirt, and old-fashioned black lace-up shoes as ugly as mine. But her hands were startling: her fingernails were perfectly manicured with shiny red polish.

The woman stood still and stared. Slowly, suspiciously, she eyed me up and down, head to toe. I fixed my eyes on the floor to avoid her sharp gaze, waiting for her to speak.

When I raised my eyes just a little, I noticed someone standing silently behind her. A dark-haired girl, about fourteen years old, I guessed. She was eyeing me, too.

I remembered how relieved I had been when I learned that Uncle Jack and Aunt Mildred had a teenage daughter. An older cousin could help me understand America. She could become a kind of sister—maybe even like Mina.

The girl I now saw had dark eyes, the same as Aunt Mildred's, and dark hair like mine. But her hair was thicker and curlier. And she was several inches taller than I was.

This must be Dorothy, I thought. I gave her a big smile and then tried out one of my new English words. "Hello."

Dorothy didn't smile back. Instead, she mumbled something that I didn't understand.

"*Was?* What?" I asked in German. "*Was?*"

Dorothy repeated what she had said. But still I didn't understand. Aunt Mildred scowled and shook her head. *"Was?"*

I gasped, looking from Dorothy to Aunt Mildred to Uncle Jack, desperate for an explanation.

"English! English!" Aunt Mildred barked.

Uncle Jack shuddered. *"Wir sprechen hier kein Deutsch,"* he whispered to me. "We don't speak German here."

But then, after Dorothy spoke a third time, he broke Aunt Mildred's rule and translated Dorothy's first words to me: "You bathe on Tuesdays and Thursdays!"

What did she mean? I still didn't understand her, but I nodded my head as if I did. Trying to catch my breath, I bent over, opened my suitcase, and removed a sealed envelope my parents had sent. Inside, I knew, were a Star of David necklace for Dorothy and a letter for my aunt and uncle. I handed the envelope to Aunt Mildred, looking up for the first time straight into her angry face.

Her red nails ripped open the envelope. The gold chain and star, which had been my mother's, spilled out and fell on the floor. Aunt Mildred swooped down, picked it up, and slapped it on the entrance table. I knew my mother had put the necklace into the envelope for Dorothy because she had nothing else to give her. Now I wished my mother had given it to me.

Then Aunt Mildred glanced at the letter, written in

neat German script, and tossed it on the table under the lamp. "Ack! German," she said, almost spitting.

This was my introduction to Aunt Mildred's view of anything German. Later, I realized that included my uncle. Often in conversation, she would correct his accented English. "Throw the ball, not *szrow*," she would say. Or, "He is *www*ealthy, not *v*ealthy."

A few days later, when no one was around, I noticed that the necklace was sitting on Dorothy's dresser. But the letter was still in the envelope on the table. The envelope was the last thing my parents had given to me just before we left for the ship. Since I had delivered the letter, just as Vati had told me to, I didn't think he would mind if I read it now.

Gently, as I opened the envelope, I sniffed the familiar scent of our woodstove. I was home again, at least for a moment. I ached when I saw Vati's even, familiar handwriting.

*Sunday, March 6, 1938*
*Dearly Beloved Family:*
*Sad times have forced us to make a terrible choice for our daughter. As parents, we are concerned about her future well-being and happiness, her physical safety, her rearing and education. We are no longer confident that we can give her these things during these difficult times in*

Germany. So it is with heavy hearts that we must send our little girl to a foreign country. We cannot be with her, but our blessings, our thoughts, and our worries will follow her.

We must thank you from the deepest part of our hearts for your kindness and love, for opening your home and your lives to our daughter. We send her to you with the hope that you will take our daughter into your home and treat her as your own.

Though you have not known her throughout her nearly thirteen years, Edith, we hope, will bring you the pleasures of a dutiful daughter. She is a sensitive child. A parent can accomplish more in her case with praise and kindness than with criticism and severity. She wants to please. It is our deepest wish that, in time, you will love her and treat her as your own daughter.

Please do not let us wait too long to hear news from you on how she is doing in America. Our only pleasure will be to receive good reports about our daughter.

May God reward you for this good deed. With anticipation that Edith will be well and bring you joy, we are, with regards,

Yours gratefully,
Frieda and Siegmund Westerfeld

Carefully, using the sleeve of the new blouse that Mutti had made for me, I soaked up my tears from the page, trying not to smudge the ink. I put the letter back, exactly as

I had found it. For days, it sat in the same spot under the lamp. Finally, when it was clear that no one wanted it, I took it and stuck it in the fold of my passport.

I reread the letter often, thinking about the words "take our daughter into your home and treat her as your own." If only that had happened.

It wasn't long before a line appeared in my mind, separating everything that had happened to me before I stepped into Aunt Mildred's apartment from everything after. On board the *Deutschland*, in New York, on the *20th Century Limited*—I had missed my family terribly, but those weeks had seemed in some ways like an adventure. The unknown was frightening, but it brought me new friends and new experiences. A door to a different world was opening up. Anything was possible.

When I arrived at Aunt Mildred's, the adventure ended. The door that had begun to open slammed shut.

One of the first evenings after I arrived, Uncle Jack answered the phone and handed it to me. "I wish I could have met you at the train," Betty said in German. "The phone lines were tied up and when Uncle Jack tried to call to tell me when you were coming in, he couldn't get through." Then she quickly added, "We should speak in English. That way you'll learn faster."

But I didn't want to speak to Betty in English. That wasn't how I knew her. Besides, I didn't understand enough to say much. I wanted the closeness and comfort of our old language. That's how I knew my sister: in German and in Germany.

"I have this wonderful new sister," Betty told me. "Her name is Deborah, but I call her Debbie. She reminds me of you."

"Sorry, I don't understand," I said. That was the English sentence I used most. "*Bitte sprich Deutsch, Betty*. Speak German please, Betty."

As a favor, she repeated the sentence in German and then continued in English. "Maybe Uncle Jack can bring you here one day and you can meet my sister, Debbie."

"*Sie ist nicht deine Schwester*. She is not your sister," I said. Often, during my first weeks in Chicago, I asked Uncle Jack to take me to see Betty, who lived about an hour away. When he asked Aunt Mildred, there was always a reason he couldn't. It was too far. They were too busy. I had too much homework or housework to give up a day for the visit.

It was more than a month before I finally got to see Betty. One Saturday, she took several buses and appeared at Aunt Mildred's apartment with an early gift for my thirteenth birthday. I was thrilled that she remembered. She brought me a new, easy-to-read German–English dictionary and a magazine for teens called *The American Girl*.

When I first saw Betty, I hardly recognized her. She was so grown-up. We spoke half in German, half in English, not comfortable with either language.

"Tiddy . . . I mean Edith." Betty said my name like an American.

"Betty." Her name was the same in German and English I hugged her hard and then stepped back to look at her. "You . . . you look so different." She had a new hairstyle—shorter and carefully curled—and she wore stylish eyeglasses now. She was tall and slender.

"You look different, too," she said.

I was happy to see Betty, but I didn't know where to begin. She never stopped talking about her foster sister, Debbie, who was taking dance classes and teaching Betty to swing and jitterbug.

"I learned the Lambeth Walk on the ship coming here," I told Betty, eager to share her new interest in dancing.

"Oh, Debbie taught me that one, too," she said. "But she doesn't do that dance anymore. Now she's doing the jitterbug."

I didn't know what to say to this new Betty. We shared nothing in the present, and it was too painful to speak of the past. The old jokes from our childhood, the friends we remembered, our parents, even Germany itself—all seemed far away.

What hit me hardest, I suppose, was the knowledge that no one at Aunt Mildred's wanted me. I had known I would have to adjust to someone else's house, with different rules and expectations. But I could not adjust to Aunt Mildred. From the moment I walked into the apartment, she made it clear that I was not her daughter, not even *her* niece.

One afternoon a couple of weeks after I arrived, when I was just beginning to understand English, Aunt Mildred called me into the dining room.

"Did you eat a piece of fruit out of the fruit bowl?" she asked, holding up a shiny red apple. I couldn't understand what she was saying until she acted it out, pretending she was about to take a bite, then pointing her finger at me.

"No!" I shook my head.

"Well," she said, "I put four apples here yesterday and now there are only three." She held up four fingers and then folded her pinky so that only three fingers remained.

I shrugged, not knowing what I was supposed to say.

"Fruit is expensive, you know," she said. "You go to the grocery store with me. You know what things cost."

This was true. Almost every day after school, Aunt Mildred expected me to meet her at the corner market, so I could carry her grocery bags to the apartment. That meant that I couldn't join any after-school activities. I went with the hope that I might run into Julius at the neighborhood store one day. After all, he lived somewhere on the South Side of Chicago, and maybe he picked up a few items for his mother. But I never found him there.

Instead, it was the same scene every time I went to the store. When the cashier told Aunt Mildred what she owed, she would click her tongue in disgust, as if the total were the cashier's fault. When she didn't have enough bills in her wallet to pay for everything, she searched her pockets and poked around the bottom of her purse for coins. If she didn't find any change, she would set aside a few items and, waving her hand, tell me to put them back on the shelves. "Don't let anyone see you," she would mutter.

Whatever she bought, I would haul to the apartment, walking all seven blocks a few steps behind Aunt Mildred, who carried nothing but her purse. I was loaded down with books written in a language I barely understood, plus two or three bags full of food I'd never seen before—things like Spam and Bisquick and cornflakes.

This was Aunt Mildred's little act. Times were hard during the Great Depression and most people didn't have money, but I could see that Aunt Mildred wanted to appear wealthy. With me carrying her groceries like a servant, she could pretend to be something she wasn't, even for just a few minutes a day. Eventually I guessed that this was why she kept her fingernails so carefully manicured. Once, I heard her tell Uncle Jack that she always had her nails done as a teenager, when she lived with her parents on Lake Shore Drive, and she wasn't about to give up her dollar-a-week manicure now.

"Each apple costs a nickel," she would tell me whenever she suspected I had eaten a piece of fruit from the bowl. "We really can't afford that."

I got the message, even if I didn't always understand the words. What Aunt Mildred meant was that she couldn't afford to feed me. So I learned never to go near the fruit bowl, never to snack between meals, never to ask for seconds at dinner.

Aunt Mildred hardly ever spoke to me, except to give orders. Even my daily list of tasks was written, not spoken: "Scrub toilets, dust bookshelves, sweep kitchen floor, wash windows, take out garbage." These orders were some of the first words I learned in English.

I was not allowed in either of the apartment's two bedrooms, except to clean. My bed was the couch in the dining room and the only space I could call my own was a shelf and the floor of the linen closet, where Aunt Mildred told me to put all my things. Since I didn't have a room of my own, I never knew what to do with myself when I wasn't cleaning or sleeping; I didn't even know where to sit to do homework.

I went to sleep only after Uncle Jack cleared the table of the paperwork he brought home from the umbrella factory where he was an accountant. Many evenings he worked late, sending out bills to department stores and luggage shops, while I sat in an uncomfortable corner chair that no one else ever used. Sometimes, I would watch Uncle Jack work and see my father at the kitchen table, adding numbers or keeping his sales records. Sometimes I would doze with a book in my lap, waiting for

Uncle Jack to finish. I wondered what we would do if my parents and Oma Sarah ever got here. I couldn't imagine where seven of us would sleep in Aunt Mildred's cramped apartment.

One word I heard from the moment I arrived was "greenhorn," a name Aunt Mildred and Dorothy called me when I wore even my best clothes from Germany, or tried to speak English, or asked questions about life in America. I knew it was no compliment and sensed it meant that I had just arrived here, but months went by before I realized that "greenhorn" was a mean, insulting name for a newcomer who is easily fooled and unfamiliar with American ways.

When Aunt Mildred saw my favorite red embroidered blouse—the one my mother had made me just before I left Germany—she waved a hand impatiently, showing me that I was to take it off and hand it over to her.

"You look like a *greenhorn* in that thing," she said. "You look like you're from Russia or some other godforsaken, backward place."

I cringed to hear her tone, even though I didn't completely understand her words. When I did as she asked and handed her my beautiful shirt, she crumpled it up and tossed it in the garbage. Shocked and hurt, I decided immediately to hide my other, white blouse. I couldn't stand to think of her throwing away something that I had brought from home, something that Mutti had made, one of the few things I could call my own.

"Greenhorn," I thought resentfully, was a word Mrs. Goldstein never would have used. Mrs. Goldstein was from the Jewish Children's Bureau, and she visited me every other month to see how I was adjusting to my new life. She brought me used clothes, took care of my medical and dental needs, and once in a while took me to special events for immigrant children.

I liked Mrs. Goldstein and looked forward to her visits. She was the only person here who seemed to care about me. When I first arrived, I didn't understand her words, but I felt her warmth. She was about my mother's age and told me that she had two teenage sons.

"I wish I had a daughter like you," she would tell me, tucking my hair behind my ear. Each time she visited, I wished that I could go home with her.

On her third visit, she brought a doctor. Mrs. Goldstein insisted on staying in the room while the doctor examined me, so that I wouldn't feel uncomfortable. Sure enough, he asked questions that embarrassed me.

"Have you had your monthly yet?"

*"Mon-ats-regel,"* Mrs. Goldstein said awkwardly. She didn't speak German, but she must have looked up the word for this conversation.

My face tingled with a red blush of embarrassment. I looked to Mrs. Goldstein to see if I had to answer him. She gently nodded.

"No." I squirmed.

"Do you know what I am talking about?" he pressed.

Mrs. Goldstein nodded again.

"Yes," I whispered, glad that Mrs. Goldstein was right next to me.

As much as I liked Mrs. Goldstein, Aunt Mildred seemed to hate her. At first, I couldn't understand why she dreaded Mrs. Goldstein's visits. In time, I realized that Aunt Mildred was afraid that I might tell this outsider something my aunt wouldn't want her to know.

"What did she ask you?" Aunt Mildred asked after each visit.

"She asked if I'm happy and I'm treated well."

"And what did you tell her?" Aunt Mildred pressed.

"Nothing, really."

"Did you say you are happy here?"

"I told her that I miss home."

"Did she ask you about your chores?"

"Yes," I said. "I told her that I have to do lots of things to help around the house."

"Did she ask what you have to do?"

This line of questioning would go on for some time. In fact, these were the longest conversations Aunt Mildred and I ever had. Otherwise, we talked only about where I was going, when I'd be back, and what housework I had to do.

It was years before I learned why Aunt Mildred was so worried about what I told Mrs. Goldstein. The Jewish

Children's Bureau paid forty-eight dollars a month to families that took in refugee children. If Mrs. Goldstein was not satisfied with the care Aunt Mildred provided, Aunt Mildred would lose the money—not to mention my household services. I'm not sure if Uncle Jack and Aunt Mildred could have paid their rent without that money from the Bureau. They certainly couldn't have afforded Aunt Mildred's manicurist.

I spoke the truth to Mrs. Goldstein. I did miss home . . . deeply. Some days, I'd sit on the couch in the dining room and cover my eyes to block out where I actually was. I ached to hear Mina's laugh when I tickled her or when she sneezed *Schweinehunde*. I longed for Mutti's voice calling my name as I played in the garden.

Every night, when I crawled into bed on that couch, I'd walk in my mind through my parents' house in Germany. I'd go from room to room, running my fingers along the old furniture that had been handed down from generation to generation, picturing where the pots and cooking utensils were kept in the kitchen, trying to remember the colors of the paintings that hung in the living room and the titles of the books on the shelves.

At night, my past rushed back to me. It was both terrifying and comforting. Often, tears soaked my pillowcase. I'd close my eyes and feel the water rolling beneath my bed and the sea-sickening rocking of the boat bringing me here.

When I could hear the voices of those I loved in my mind, I was relieved that I had not lost them yet, that they were still alive within me. Then I would give myself a little speech, in German, using the very same words I knew my father would say.

"We will all be together again," I would tell myself. "It won't be too long."

"Be patient, Tiddy," Vati would say. "Be patient."

*Nimm jeden Tag so wie er kommt.*

"Take each day as it comes."

## 8

# BABY BEAR'S CHAIR

**B**ut it wasn't so easy to "take each day as it comes," especially school days. I spent my first morning at O'Keefe Elementary School in the principal's office. After he introduced me to a few of my new thirteen-year-old classmates, the students returned to their class and the principal marched me down the hall, to the very last classroom at the end of the corridor. There, the teacher sat on a chair before a class of little children.

"This is red," she said slowly, holding up a flash card with a word and a color on it. "R-E-D. Spell it with me, class. That's right. Red."

They had put me in first grade, and they might as well have put a dunce cap on my head. If I had to be in first grade, I thought, at least I should have gotten a *Schultüte*— a "school cone" of rolled-up paper filled with candy, fruit, and chocolate that German parents give to their first graders on the first day of school to make it special. It would have been strange to get one in March, but no stranger than being put back six grades.

I was small for my age, but not as small as a first grader, and I could never fit in one of their desks. The only large chair was the teacher's, so I had to sit on a tiny chair made for six-year-olds. My knees poked out from the seat like a camel's humps. When some older kids looked through the window in the door and saw me on that miniature chair, at the back of a room decorated with large alphabet letters and primary colors, they started calling me Goldilocks. I learned later she was the girl who broke Baby Bear's chair in "The Three Bears."

My first-grade class began each day by reciting the Pledge of Allegiance. The children stood facing the flag and lifted their right arms straight out in front of their bodies, palms down, while saying the pledge. Watching them, I gasped, remembering when students in my German classroom started using the Nazi salute, just about the time the neighbors beat up my father.

The first-grade teacher tried to explain what she expected of me. She placed her hand on her heart and then held it out to the flag and called out words like "allegiance" and "United States of America." I gathered that she was trying to show me that by saying the pledge and saluting the flag, I was loyal to this country.

To me, that was ridiculous. I didn't understand a word

of the pledge; I didn't understand anything about the United States or what the flag was supposed to mean. And I would never have given that salute back in Germany. It represented everything that threatened my family. Why would I do it here?

The next day I stayed in my seat when it was time for the pledge. The teacher walked over and insisted that I get out of my tiny chair. When I was standing, she firmly lifted my arm and held my hand straight out toward the red, white, and blue flag. All the children stared at us in silence until the teacher began reciting the pledge loudly. The children chimed in while I resisted.

". . . to the flag of the United States of America and to . . ."

"*Ich will das nicht tun.* I don't want to do this." I squirmed, trying to get the teacher to loosen her grip on my arm.

"*Das ist nicht meine Fahne.* This is not my flag."

". . . one nation, indivisible . . ."

"*Lassen Sie mich los.* Let me go."

". . . and justice for all."

"*Ich möchte zurück nach Deutschland.* I want to go back to Germany." "*Ich will nach Hause.* I want to go home."

I was not happy in school, but I worked hard and was learning English fast. I discovered I had a gift for languages. As I started learning to read English, I was introduced to the perfect American family in the simple books that were used to teach reading. Here Dick and Jane and their dog, Spot, had one adventure after another. Grownups never yelled, and night never fell. Dick and Jane played hour after hour, day after day, as if childhood were an endless summer afternoon—nothing like my life at Aunt Mildred's. I dreamed of living in Dick and Jane's world.

If I couldn't be Jane, I wanted to be Evelyn, one of my first-grade classmates. Evelyn's mother looked a little like Mrs. Goldstein, with brownish blond hair and warm brown eyes. I had never seen anyone, except maybe Mina, who smiled and laughed as much as Evelyn's mother. She walked Evelyn to school every morning and returned every afternoon to walk her home. This didn't seem unusual to six-year-old Evelyn, who had never known anything else. But I hung on every smile, every hug, the slightest touch that passed between Evelyn and her mother. They never knew that my ears were always turned toward their conversations and my eyes followed every move they made, as if I could drink in the love I needed just by watching them.

About a month after I entered first grade, my English had improved enough that I was moved up to third grade. I had been the teacher's helper in first grade; the younger children had looked up to me and didn't know enough to tease me. But third graders weren't so accepting.

"Welcome, Edith," Mrs. Gallagher, my new teacher, said as she showed me to an extra chair in the back of the room. The desks in third grade fit no better than those back in first grade.

"Class," she continued, "let's say hello to our new classmate, Edith Westerfeld. She is from a country in Europe called Germany. She traveled all the way across the Atlantic Ocean to come to America." Someone giggled. Then a few kids mumbled, "Hello."

One of the small comforts I found in third grade was that we continued to read about Dick and Jane's adventures. The pages of the book were the only predictable, stable world I knew, where no one corrected my English or laughed at me.

After that, every few weeks I skipped a grade or two, allowing my seventh-grade peers to monitor my progress through teasing. "Yowsah!" they'd yell—that's how people said "Wow!" in those days. "Yowsah, she's moving up!" "Ooooohhh, she's a big fifth grader now." "Hey, Goldilocks, is that chair *juuuusssst right?*"

Not really. None of the chairs felt just right. I felt awkward in school, but even more uncomfortable about actually learning the English language. I wanted to understand my classmates and fit into the new school, but with each new word I learned in English, I felt like I was taking a step away from Germany. Away from my home and family.

Even though I had mixed feelings about learning the

language, gradually, I did understand more and more. I could read and write better than I could speak, though my accent—especially the way I pronounced the letters "r" and "th"—marked me as different. "Around *za* corn*ah*," I would say, or, "I can't remember *zis*." It gave the kids another reason to make fun of me.

I surprised everyone with how fast I was learning. Soon my English was good enough for the teachers to finally allow me into seventh grade in the last month of the school year. As I joined my classmates, a couple of the boys snickered and nudged each other.

"Dirty Kraut," one boy said in a low voice. "Dirty Jew, go back where you came from." There were a few other Jewish kids in the class, but they just kept their heads down when they heard those words.

I had arrived in time for the final class project: creating a scrapbook with family pictures and stories of our lives. I didn't want to do this project. I didn't want to give those boys any more information about my German past so they could find more ways to taunt me. Also, I imagined all the other students would bring in scrapbooks of their Dick and Jane childhoods. I had no pictures from my childhood except the two passport photos of my mother and father.

So, for the first time in my life, I didn't do my homework.

Back in Germany, I would have been too scared to skip even a single assignment. The German teachers were very strict; many walked around with a ruler, banging a desk or whacking knuckles when students misbehaved or hadn't done their homework. In America, the teachers were more understanding, especially Mrs. Gallagher and my seventh-grade teacher, Mrs. Rich. And here, they didn't threaten students with rulers.

"Edith?" Mrs. Rich called on me one afternoon after all the students had handed in their scrapbooks. "See me after school."

I was scheduled to meet Aunt Mildred at the grocery store at 3:30, and I knew I would be punished if I was late. I hoped Mrs. Rich wouldn't take long.

"Edith, why didn't you hand in the project?" she asked sternly as I approached her desk. I glanced at the clock and then bowed my head, as I would do back in Germany, to show respect. In Germany, it was considered rude to look an elder in the eye.

"Please look at me when I'm talking to you," Mrs. Rich said.

Slowly, I lifted my gaze and looked at her directly.

"Why didn't you hand in the project?" she asked again, sharply this time.

I didn't answer. I didn't want to explain.

"Edith, why didn't you do the work?" Her voice was a little softer now. Usually, Mrs. Rich was kind to me, so I decided to tell her the truth.

"I don't . . . I mean I won't tell my story," I said.

"But I know the children would like to hear it. I'm sure yours is one of the most interesting histories in the class."

"But . . . but," I blurted out, unable to stop the tears, "I different. I different."

Now Mrs. Rich's face changed. "I see, Edith. You feel that you don't fit in?"

"Yes. I have no pictures. I have nothing."

Pulling a white handkerchief from her desk drawer, Mrs. Rich looked at me kindly. "Well, maybe there is some other way that you can share your story with your classmates."

"They call me . . . they call me Kraut. Goldilocks. Or Jew, Jew, Jew."

Mrs. Rich looked like I was stabbing her as I said the word "Jew" over and over again. She always stopped the taunts when she heard them, but my classmates picked their moments when she wasn't around.

Mrs. Rich must have told Uncle Jack what I had said, because a couple of days later, he lent me his old German camera, a Leica.

"I thought you might like to take some photos," he said, with the same sweetness I had seen back at the train station. "Maybe you can use them for your class project."

"No," I said, stunned that he had thought to give it to me. "I afraid I break it."

"See how you like it." He handed it to me. I had no idea how to use it, but I carefully fingered the knobs. "I can teach you how to use it. Maybe you can send a few pictures back to Germany."

It would be wonderful to send Mutti, Vati, and Mina some photographs of Chicago, I thought, especially of Lake Michigan. Once in a while, when Aunt Mildred didn't have too many chores for me after school, I would walk along the lakefront, where the smell of the water reminded me of home and the Rhein River. Some days, I wished I could seal the thick lake smell into an envelope and mail it off to my family. A picture would be almost as good.

"Thank you," I said, and Uncle Jack flashed his crooked smile at me.

Now I was glad I had told Mrs. Rich about my classmates' name-calling and meanness.

But secretly, the one person I really wanted to talk to was Julius. I wondered why I hadn't heard from him. Maybe he didn't know how to get to Aunt Mildred's. Chicago was such a big city. How could I ever find him?

Those first months my classmates at O'Keefe saw me as easy prey. But finally, just before school ended for the summer, I found myself becoming friendly with a girl in my class named Helene Smith. Helene was much taller than I was and already, as Mrs. Goldstein's doctor would say, had her "monthly." Probably we looked like a big and a little sister together, but I didn't care; I was so happy to feel that I might have an American friend.

Helene invited me to come over one day, but Aunt Mildred said no; I had to carry her groceries after school.

Helene didn't give up. One Saturday afternoon, she actually stopped by Aunt Mildred's apartment to see me. I was thrilled, but Aunt Mildred was not.

"Who are you?" Aunt Mildred asked, peeking through the crack she'd opened at the door.

"Helene Smith." When I heard that, I went running to the door.

"What are you here for?" Aunt Mildred demanded.

"Can Edith come over to my place?" Helene smiled at me, and I waved at her from behind Aunt Mildred.

Then Uncle Jack came to see who was at the door. When he saw that it was a girlfriend, he said to Aunt Mildred, "Let her go."

"No," she said sharply. "She has chores to do today."

"She can skip one day," Uncle Jack said, in a rare moment of challenging her.

"No, she can't," Aunt Mildred said, sounding really annoyed now. "I have my mah-jongg party tonight and I have to have a clean house."

Uncle Jack sighed and turned away.

"Edith is busy," Aunt Mildred informed Helene. "She's not going out today."

Later, after Helene had left, Aunt Mildred laid down the law: I was not to spend any time with Helene, and she shouldn't come to the apartment again.

"She is much bigger than you. Maybe much older. Much more developed."

I didn't say anything. I was too confused. I couldn't imagine why that mattered.

"She's probably fast, too," Aunt Mildred added. Now I truly had no idea what she was talking about, but I knew it was no compliment. It seemed Aunt Mildred could find something wrong with anyone I might like.

So, instead of trying to make friends, I started going to the library; it was the only place where I wasn't the poor refugee girl or the Kraut or, even worse, the Jew. I could just be me and lose myself in books.

And there, I got the first thing that could belong only to me: a library card. It had my name on it—"Edith Westerfeld"—though, in my mind, I still read it as "Edit Vesterfeld."

What was really important, though, was that I felt safe there. The characters in my books didn't tease me, hurt me, reject or abandon me. They were much more reliable than real people, and not even Aunt Mildred could take them away.

# 9

## STEP ON A CRACK

During my first months in America, I got just a few letters from my family. Why didn't Vati, Mutti, or even Mina write to me? I always wrote to them every Sunday, no matter what.

I lived from one letter to the next. In between, the same worries ran through my head like a broken record: Why didn't I hear from them? Were things getting worse at home? Were my parents safe? Would they ever get out?

To manage my fears, I became a deep believer—not in God, but in what I called "if . . . then." By this time, I wasn't sure I believed in God anyway. What kind of a God would make parents send their children away?

Instead, I became superstitious. I convinced myself that *if* I did certain things, *then* my parents would get out of Germany and join me. I also feared the opposite: that if I *didn't* do certain things, they would surely meet their deaths. It was like the children's sidewalk game that has only one rule: step on a crack, break your mother's back. I didn't want to step on any cracks.

But my superstitions came with lots of rules. First, according to "if . . . then," I had to do well in school. This was hard, but as I learned to speak and write English, my grades improved. Second, I had to do exactly what my parents had asked of me. "Our only pleasure will be to receive good reports about our daughter," they had written in their letter. So I was determined to be a good girl. I wasn't always sure what that meant, but I knew I was never to cause Aunt Mildred any trouble, even if that meant I never got to hang out with other kids after school or invite them over to Aunt Mildred's apartment.

During the summer, Aunt Mildred found plenty of work for me to do, but I was determined to make some money to help my parents get out of Germany. So, in the few spare hours I had, I would do what I had done in Germany—garden.

I scooped out the seeds from the tomatoes and cucumbers that were left on the dinner plates. I took ten small paper Dixie cups from the bathroom garbage can, placed seeds in them, and added water. Then I placed them on the windowsill behind the couch where I slept. After a few days, I rinsed, dried, and planted the seeds in soil in the cups, just as we used to do at home. Every day, sometimes two or three times a day, I examined the cups, looking for the first sign of growth.

*Jetzt wachs doch endlich mal.* "Come on," I'd say to the cups, "grow." In my mind, growing seeds was like growing money. In those cups, I saw my family's passage. *If* something would come up, *then* my parents could get here.

To my surprise, in just a few weeks, seven cups had seedlings. Now all I had to do was sell them. As soon as the plants looked strong and healthy, I put the cups on an old plate and knocked on doors in the apartment building.

"Would you like to buy seedlings?" I had practiced that line over and over again before approaching the neighbors, trying to say "would" without the German "v" sound. If I spoke slowly, I could control the "v" in my "w."

"We don't have time or money for gardening," said the mother of three who lived next door. She didn't even seem to notice how nicely I asked.

"Honey, we can't even come up with this month's rent," said the old lady who lived above us and always smiled at me in the hallway.

"Would you like to buy . . ." I said to a young mother carrying a baby on her hip as she opened the door to her basement apartment. Before I could tell her what I was selling, she said, "My husband just lost his job." Then she closed the door on me.

And that was that. I had a product, but I couldn't find

any customers. Uncle Jack had asked me almost every day how my garden was growing and whether I had sold any plants. When he saw that my little business had failed, he told me about another job: delivering water.

Water out of a tap wasn't clean enough to drink, so people bought well water from a pumping station. My job was to pump the well water into gallon jugs, then deliver the bottles in an old red wooden wagon to neighbors. Customers paid ten cents a bottle, money I brought back to the pumping station, but every now and then, someone would slap an extra dime—or even a quarter—into my palm. The weight of the coins in my hand was so sweet; I was convinced that "if . . . then" was working. Surely my parents would be on their way to America in a matter of months.

Uncle Jack and I made a jar for what we called the "German Immigration Fund." I put all my earnings in it, and Uncle Jack would add some change when he had any to spare. Once I had the delivery business going, my jar began to fill with shiny coins.

One day in August, when Aunt Mildred was out, I sat down on the living room floor, emptied the jar, and counted the money. I had saved $9.83. Nearly ten dollars!

I called Betty and told her about the jar.

"It's not too late, is it?" I asked, as I bit my lip.

"I guess not. Not yet. I'll try to help."

I was glad that she wanted to help, but her "not yet" made me feel like a deadly clock was ticking and there wasn't much time left.

I tried to improve my English by reading the newspaper. Every day I labored over stories with headlines like "Mud Slides in Southern California Kill 144" or "FDR Asks for Buildup of Army and Navy." I knew FDR meant President Franklin Delano Roosevelt, but mud slides and a buildup were beyond me.

It was the comics, with their funny pictures and simple words, that I really liked. And soon I discovered that I could follow the sports section, too. Uncle Jack was a big Chicago White Sox fan and I would report the box scores to him each day. I got to know the names of all the players, too—Radcliff, Walker, Kuhel, and Appling—like they were part of an exciting extended family.

When the baseball season ended, I kept reading the newspaper, trying to figure out from front-page stories what was going on in Germany. It was still hard to understand, but finally, in late fall of 1938, I got a glimpse of what life was like for Mutti, Vati, Oma Sarah, and Mina. But it didn't come from the newspapers. Instead, I saw motion pictures of Germany on the big screen one Saturday afternoon, when I had the rare chance to go to the movies with Dorothy and her friends.

Most of the time, Dorothy didn't take much interest in me, but a few of her girlfriends did. To them, I was Dorothy's poor little refugee cousin. I suppose they felt sorry for me, especially when Dorothy was mean, teasing me in front of them about my clumsy English and heavy German accent.

On this afternoon, Dorothy's friends had gathered at the apartment to go see a movie called *Test Pilot*.

"Why don't you come with us?" a girl named Alice said to me. I looked at Dorothy. She looked away.

"Yes, Edith, you should come along," another girl said. "Clark Gable is such a dream. He's starring with Myrna Loy and Spencer Tracy. It will be fun."

Dorothy groaned. "Go ask," she said, without even looking at me.

When I told Aunt Mildred that all my chores were done and Dorothy had asked me to go to the movies, she surprised me and said I could go. Did she want the apartment all to herself? Whatever the reason, it was worth taking fifteen cents from the German Immigration Fund to pay for my ticket. This was the first time I had ever dipped into the jar.

"Tiddy!" I heard my father's stern voice in my head as I removed two coins. I felt as if he had slapped my hand.

"Just this one time, Vati," I said out loud. "And no popcorn or treats."

All Dorothy's friends were tall, like she was. As we

walked the five blocks to the theater, I was breathless, trying to keep pace.

"Don't take such little steps," Dorothy yelled back at
me.

Even though I had fallen behind, I could still hear what
the girls were saying.

"I love Clark Gable's eyes," said Dorothy. "And those
eyebrows really set them off."

"Actually," Alice said, "I think Spencer Tracy is a hunk
of heartbreak. He has such a dreamy smile."

"But he's so short," Dorothy protested. "The magazines
say he has to stand on a box to kiss his leading ladies."

As we settled into our soft seats, I felt the old excitement of being at the movies. I was so happy that I hadn't
had to sneak into a darkened theater and I could be with a
group of girls rather than sitting in the back by myself.
Waiting for the lights to dim and the show to begin, Alice
offered me some of her buttered popcorn.

"Spencer Tracy seems so real to me," she said. "When
you watch him on the screen, it feels like he's talking just
to you." I couldn't wait for the movie to begin so that I
could see for myself whether I liked Spencer Tracy or
Clark Gable better.

But before the feature started, a newsreel came on
broadcasting the news of the world.

*"Here in Berlin, it is November 8, nine-thirty a.m.,"* said the
reporter. I jumped when I heard the word "Berlin." Imme-

diately, I tuned in, leaning forward so I wouldn't miss a word of what he was saying. *"I have just spent eight horrendous hours following Nazi storm troopers in what will probably prove to be the worst pogrom in Europe's history. Lootings, vandalism, and burning of synagogues have taken place all over Berlin in a night that is now being called Kristallnacht . . ."*

My mind raced. My heart pounded. My hands began to shake. Pictures flashed on the screen of synagogues in flames and Nazi soldiers with clubs beating up old Jewish men and women, their bodies lying in the streets. I saw Jewish shops with shattered windows and merchandise tossed onto the sidewalks. One of those shops could have been my father's store. One of those bodies could have been Vati lying in the street. Or Mutti. Or Oma Sarah.

*"The leading German rabbi, Dr. Leo Baeck, has just told me, 'We have no place to go. Nobody wants us.'"*

How would my family ever get out?

When the main feature came on the screen, I couldn't bear to watch it. Who cared whether Clark Gable or Spencer Tracy was more handsome? For two hours, I couldn't stop thinking about home.

Maybe, I thought, this was happening only in Berlin. Stockstadt was just a small village, far away from the big cities. Maybe the Nazis wouldn't bother with Stockstadt. There were only three Jews there anyway—Mutti, Vati, and Oma Sarah.

Still, I couldn't be sure.

Dorothy and the other girls didn't say anything about the newsreel as we left the theater. But after the girls went their separate ways, Dorothy slowed to walk with me for the last few blocks.

"Have you gotten a letter from your parents lately?" she asked.

She had never shown any interest before, but now she pressed. "When was the last time you heard from them?"

Suddenly, I began to walk faster as I tried to remember. Dorothy had to take a few quick steps to catch up with me.

"Not for a few months," I told her.

"Are they okay? What do they say?"

"The same. In every letter they say they are trying to get their exit papers together."

"Any luck?"

I swallowed hard, taking my time to answer. "I guess not," I finally said as we turned onto the apartment's walkway. "It's hard to know."

I didn't think Dorothy was aware of the German Immigration Fund, but later that evening, while I was sitting on the living room couch reading the *Chicago Daily News*, I looked up to see her standing next to the small table near the linen closet where I kept my glass jar. She was staring at it. Was she going to take some money out? I saw her reach into her pocket. With a *clink-clink*, she dropped several coins into my jar. Then, without a word, she went into her room.

A few days after I saw the newsreel, Uncle Jack began making dozens of phone calls. Every spare minute, he sat at the dining room table, dialing someone. At first, I had no idea what he was doing or why, but it soon became clear.

"This raffle is the only way that we can raise money to get the family out of Germany," I heard him say into the phone. "It is a vorthy cause."

"*Wwwww*aaaa. *Wwww*aaa," Aunt Mildred corrected his accent, as she always did. "Like *wwww*ater." Uncle Jack covered the receiver with his hand.

"Vatever you can afford vould be a big help. Und you might be the vinner."

"*Wwww*aaa, like water." She thumped the heel of her hand on her forehead as if that would bang it into Uncle Jack's head.

Holding the receiver in one hand and keeping a finger on each name in the synagogue directory, Uncle Jack was calling everyone in it.

I didn't know any of these people; I had found any excuse not to go to synagogue with Aunt Mildred and Uncle Jack. The few times I went, I felt like a fake praying

132

to God. And the place made me miss my old congregation and my family.

One evening, Uncle Jack hung up the phone, turned to me, and said, "That was your old rabbi, Rabbi Rubenstein from Crumstadt. Did you know that he just joined our congregation?"

"He did? That's great!" I said. "Does he know anything about my parents?"

"I asked, but he didn't have any news. But he asked all about you—'How is Tiddy? When will I see her at temple?' "

I looked away. How could I bear to see him? It would just make me sad that he was here and my family was not.

"The rabbi bought five tickets for our raffle," Uncle Jack added.

But most of his telephone conversations ended the same way: "Vell, okay, yes, I understand. Maybe you know of some jobs for them? They're very hardworking. Yes, I know these are tough times for all of us."

Since Uncle Jack was selling tickets to get "the family" out of Germany, I thought maybe he knew somehow that things were getting worse for them. I waited even more anxiously for a letter. Then finally, a letter did come. It was addressed to Uncle Jack, not to me.

I was dying to read the letter, but I knew I shouldn't. And, if I read it, I would be violating my "if . . . then" rules not to do anything wrong. That could endanger my parents' lives.

Day after day, I eyed the letter on the table. Every time I looked at it, I was tempted to read it. One day, I picked it up to feel its weight in my hand. It was several pages long. Maybe something had happened. It could be terrible news. If I read it, I was afraid of what I might learn, but I was burning to know what it said.

Finally, one afternoon when no one was home, I picked up the envelope, which had been opened, and peered inside at my mother's familiar neat handwriting. Gently, I removed the thin tissue paper inside so no one could tell that I had touched it.

*Darmstadt*
*December 18, 1938*
*Dear Jakob,*

*You write that it is your wish that we should be together with our children. But now, after Kristallnacht, it is more difficult to get out.*

*I was forced to leave our home in Stockstadt three weeks ago. Now I am living in an apartment building in Darmstadt with six other Jews from nearby villages. An SS guard watches the apartment day and night and sometimes the six of us must do work at local factories.*

*You asked me about how your brother is doing. Sorry*

*to say, dear Siegmund was taken to the Sachsenhausen Labor Camp a few months ago and I don't hear from him often . . .*

"Oh my God!" I gasped, accidentally dropping the letter. "Vati is in a camp!" I picked up the letter and continued reading.

*. . . Lately it is cold here so the mail is slow. But Sieg-mund wrote me three times about a month ago, asking, "Have you heard anything? Is there anyone, anywhere in the world who can line up work for us so that we can get sponsorship?" We can't leave Germany without sponsor-ship and we can't get sponsorship without lining up a job somewhere first. And I can't sell the house unless all of our papers are in order.*

*I have written all the relatives, begging for help. From Bertha in Uruguay, I haven't had any letters since Octo-ber. Martin in Palestine hasn't written since July. Sarah's brother, Moses, who lives in America, has not sent a letter since last May. I know you keep looking for work for us in Chicago. Any news yet?*

*I wrote to my second cousin on my mother's side, Setta, to see if her uncle could help. Even our dear Betty has tried to contact our cousins who moved to America years ago about jobs. But so far, nothing.*

*Yes, dear Jakob, I have my worries. We are trapped here. I wish all the relatives could get together and figure out what to do for us.*

*I am glad to hear that Dorothy had such a beautiful report card. You must be so proud of her.*

*We keep hoping to be together with our children. No one can imagine what this is like. I hurt every day. A divided life is only half a life; I open the door and no one is there.*

> *Kisses for all of you, my dear ones.*
>
> *Your Frieda*

## 10

## DON'T CALL ME JULIUS!

Usually, the letters I received from Europe were written on blue, tissue-thin airmail stationery. I spotted them easily among the bills on Aunt Mildred's letter table. But one day I noticed a regular white envelope with a U.S. postage stamp and it was addressed to me.

My heart jumped. Who would write me? Gertie? It had been a whole year and she still hadn't sent me a letter, and I didn't have her address. Then I realized it couldn't be Gertie because the return address was from Alabama.

*Peter!* I ripped the envelope, hardly able to open it fast enough. The letter was two pages long, written in a neat German hand.

March 20, 1939
Birmingham, Alabama
Dear Edith,

I promised I'd write to you and here I am. It has been a whole year, but I haven't forgotten you. So much has happened since we got off the Deutschland!

After I left New York, I traveled by train with a man from a Jewish organization to Birmingham, Alabama. When we got to Washington, D.C., the white people stayed in their seats, but the colored passengers moved to the back coaches. The man said something about Jim Crow, but I didn't know what he was talking about.

Now that I live in Alabama, I know that Jim Crow is a bunch of laws that make colored people have separate water fountains, bathrooms, and schools. It's just like home, Edith. Remember the signs that said, "No Jews Allowed"?

But I am writing you with good news. I want to tell you that after months of waiting at an orphanage, I have been adopted! I was the last of nineteen children. Each time a family would come to adopt someone, I would clean myself up, comb my hair, make my bed nice and tight, and try to make the people think that I would be a good son.

I think more than thirty couples came and asked me questions like "Where did you come from?" and "How old are you?" and "Do you have any hobbies?" I felt like I was put up for sale. People were looking at me the way they might pick out potatoes at the greengrocer.

Nobody picked me. I wondered what was wrong with me and why they didn't want me. I think they didn't want someone who was sixteen years old. This hurt me as much as anything that had happened before. Even saying good-bye to my parents in Germany.

But a month ago, my American cousins who live in Birmingham learned that they could adopt me. They have a son my age and they want him to learn German. So now, I have someplace to be.

How do you like America? I hope you have a good home with your aunt and uncle. At least you had a place to go once you got here.

Please write me at the new address on the envelope. Do you ever hear from Gertie or see Julius?

Yours,

Peter

P.S. Write me.
P.P.S. Soon.
P.P.P.S. In case you don't have Julius's address, I'm sending it to you here.


I was so excited about Peter's letter! I still hadn't heard from Julius, but I wanted to share Peter's news with him. Now I had his address, which Peter had included on a separate slip of paper. Every day I still thought about Julius. Would this be the day he would phone me? Or appear at Aunt Mildred's door? But these things never happened.

Finally, I decided that I would find Julius—even if he hadn't found me. I looked on a map and discovered that his house was only six miles away from Aunt Mildred's apartment. Six miles! That was a good distance, but not so far away as my sister Betty on the north side of Chicago, or Peter in Alabama. Or my family in Germany.

I was determined to find Julius, but I had no idea how I would get there. The streetcar didn't go near his house. I couldn't ask Uncle Jack to drive me in his brother-in-law's car; he only borrowed it on weekends to run important errands. Besides, he would never take me to a boy's house. Back home in Germany, it would have been easy. There I had a blue bicycle that I rode everywhere. But here, the only way to get around was walking or taking the streetcar. Or sometimes roller skating.

So I decided. After finishing my chores on a Saturday, I would strap on Dorothy's hand-me-down roller skates and skate to Julius's house.

The night before my adventure, I waited until everyone had gone to bed. Then I turned on the living room lamp, took out my map, and studied it to figure out the most direct route from Aunt Mildred's apartment.

The next morning, I rushed through all my chores. The kitchen floor probably wasn't clean enough for Aunt Mildred, but she wasn't around to inspect. So I tucked into my jacket pocket my map and a Baby Ruth candy bar I had been saving for a special occasion, put on my skates, and started out.

Six miles was farther than I had imagined. After only a few blocks, I felt worlds away. Apartment buildings like Aunt Mildred's gave way to large redbrick houses with impressive front lawns. Every few blocks, I stopped, pulled out my map, and made sure I was still on the route I had marked in red pen. I didn't want to waste any of my roller skating energy getting lost.

I found a path that ran along the lake and stayed on it for a while. Rhythmically moving and looking out at the water, I could almost imagine that none of this had happened, that I was still in Stockstadt, that I would go home later to find Vati behind the store counter taking money from Fräulein Krugg, our neighbor; Mutti scrubbing carrots with feathery green tops in the deep kitchen sink; and Oma Sarah sitting on her favorite kitchen chair knitting argyle socks

Then I remembered Julius. If none of this had happened, I wouldn't be on my way to see him. Would he be glad to see me? Would he put his arm around me again? I picked up speed.

A half hour later, I finally arrived at a house whose number matched the address Peter had sent me. My heart pounded from exercise and excitement. I leaned my hands onto my knees to catch my breath. Then I stared up at the house. It had a wide porch surrounding its oak front door and large windows. This, I realized, was a very nice home.

I combed my hair with my fingers, wiped the sweat from my forehead with my jacket sleeve, and kneeled down to take off my skates. But before I had the chance, a boy came running out the front door and down the steps. When he saw me, he stopped and stared.

"Hello?" he called out, as if he didn't recognize me.

Was it Julius? This boy was taller than Julius. He wore brown corduroy knickers buckled below the knee, with a matching jacket and high brown socks that came up to the edge of his knickers. It was the latest American fashion. The only thing he was wearing that didn't match was a Chicago White Sox baseball cap.

*"Guten Tag,"* I said, figuring that if this was Julius, speaking in German would refresh his memory. He took another step toward me, then stopped again.

"Edith." His voice had changed as much as his appearance. It was much lower and now it sounded cold. And he had called me Edi*th*. Not E-Edit. Or even Edit.

"Hello," he said in English. "What are *you* doing here?"

"Julius?" I said, as if to ask, Is that you?

"No," he said in English. "Don't call me Julius. I'm Jerry now."

*"Aber du bist doch der Julius aus Köln in Deutschland.* But you're Julius," I insisted, still speaking in German. "From Cologne in Germany."

"That's all gone now," he answered in English, waving his hand as if to brush away everything I knew about him. "I don't need to think about the past. I'm an American now."

He placed both hands on the rim of his baseball cap to straighten it on his head. "Good to see you, Edith, but I gotta go now." I hadn't fully caught my breath when he said, "I'm on my way to meet some friends. Sorry."

As I took off my jacket and tied it around my waist, I decided not to tell him about Peter's letter. He seemed to have no interest in me. Why would he care about Peter? In just a few words, Julius—Jerry—had erased everything I had known about him. Maybe he had decided not to be Jewish anymore, too.

I felt hot and sweaty; I knew my face must be all red. I was still confused, but I understood. I could not be this boy's friend.

I stiffly held up my flat hand, but I did not wave. "*Auf Wiedersehen.* Goodbye," I said in German. *Auf Wiedersehen, Julius.*

I turned on my skates and rolled back the way I had come.

I was back at Aunt Mildred's apartment in half the time it had taken me to reach Julius's house. When I sat down on the steps to take off my skates, my face was damp and flushed, my blouse soaked in sweat.

Exhausted, I pushed myself up the two flights, carrying my skates into the empty apartment. As I placed them on the floor of the tiny linen closet, I saw my old doll Arno on the shelf leaning against the back wall. Months ago, when I had first come to Aunt Mildred's, I had placed him there.

I took Arno off the shelf and covered my face with his ragged body. I breathed deeply, inhaling the wood-burning smell that brought back the warmth of sitting with my parents in our living room in Germany.

Then I gently put Arno back on the shelf and looked around me at the strange, cramped apartment: the holey cane chair in the hallway, the dreary yellow wallpaper in the kitchen, the worn couch in the dining room where I slept. The stillness of the apartment choked me.

I could not describe, even to Mina if she had been there, my loneliness. For the first time, I grasped that I was truly on my own. I could depend on no one. There was no one to share my struggles and hopes. Not even Julius. No one to tell about my awful visit with Julius. Nobody even knew who he was.

But even though I was alone, I was sure that one day Mutti and Vati would come. Somehow they would find a way. Then I would no longer be under Aunt Mildred's rule. Meanwhile, I thought, I shouldn't expect much from Aunt Mildred, Dorothy, or even Uncle Jack.

This was not my home.

## 11

## HANKUS PANKUS

We're going to have a party next Thursday for Dorothy's birthday," Aunt Mildred said to me one hot August afternoon. "I would appreciate it if you would find something to do."

"To do?" I said, confused. "You mean at the party?"

"No," she said, annoyed.

"You want me to help?"

"No!" She sliced the air with her painted red finger-nails. "You don't need to be around."

Then I understood: they didn't want me at the party. I wasn't part of the "we." They didn't even want me to help serve the cake.

I tried to make the best of it. At least I would get a day of freedom! For months I had thought, if only I could have a day without chores, without Aunt Mildred's rules, a day I could choose to do whatever I want. But I'd always stop myself. That'll never happen, I'd tell myself. Don't even think about it.

But now, I *had* to think about it. For Dorothy's birthday, I was being given the gift of a day. What would I do with it?

I could go to the library, though that seemed pointless since that's where I went whenever I had a spare moment. I should think bigger. How about visiting the Museum of Science and Industry? Someone had told me that one exhibit showed a street in America at the turn of the century. I was curious to see it, but I knew that the first-year high school students went there and I could wait for that field trip. I could go downtown to Marshall Field's on State Street, but I'd been there once when Aunt Mildred needed someone to carry her shopping bags. I thought about the zoo, but it reminded me of that poor, broken boy on the boat.

Then I had an idea. I looked in the newspaper to see if the White Sox would be in town that day. They were home, playing the Detroit Tigers. Wasn't Hank Greenberg a Tiger? I remembered reading about him because he was one of the few Jewish baseball players in the major leagues. I looked at the paper and noticed that every Thursday was Ladies' Day. I could go to the game without spending a dime! And I could see Hank Greenberg play ball!

On Wednesday evening, I got out my map of the South Side of Chicago, then folded it carefully to show Comiskey Park. I planned my adventure, just as I had planned my route to Julius's house, only this time in black ink. I would take the South Side streetcar and get off at 35th Street.

I set out early and arrived at the stadium by noon, long before batting practice had begun. Even though the game wouldn't start for a few hours, the street in front of Comiskey Park was already as crowded and noisy as any I'd seen in New York City. Peddlers were yelling the same words over and over, hawking peanuts, team yearbooks, scorecards, and colorful team pennants. People were rushing to the gates, elbowing past each other in such a hurry that I was a little scared.

All around me, I heard different languages—English, of course, and Polish, which I recognized, and others I had never heard before. When someone called out *"Beeil Dich!"*—"Hurry up!"—I felt dizzy, suddenly confused about where I was.

I hadn't been in a crowd like this since Ellis Island. And this place smelled the same: smoky and sweaty.

Just outside the gates, young boys wearing white shirts and ties lined up, trying to catch the eye of every passing man. I stood next to them, trying to figure out what they were doing. First, the boys looked at the man's hands. If he had a ticket, the boys put on big smiles, greeting him with a friendly "Good day, sir," or "Go Sox!" or "We'll stop the Hankus Pankus." I had no idea what they were talking about.

"Hey mister, hey mister," all the boys were shouting. "Pick me! Pick me!"

Now and then, a man would point to one of the boys, who would jump up. "Yowsah!" he would shriek, and follow the man into the ballpark. Eventually, I figured out that an adult who had paid for a ticket could bring a child into the park for free. The boys didn't bother approaching women because this was Ladies' Day—no tickets needed for ladies. It was the men who could offer these boys a chance to see the game.

Some of the boys standing next to me were talking about Greenberg. "Did you know that he nearly beat the record of sixty home runs last year?" one boy asked.

"Yeah, and did you know that he's a Jew?" another answered.

I cringed when he said the word "Jew."

"Yeah. Who ever heard of a Jewish baseball player?"

"Just think," said a third boy, who was munching on a Hershey's chocolate bar. "If he ever beats the home run record, they'd have to make his candy bar kosher!"

I followed one boy and his ticket holder through the gate and into a dark passageway. At the end, I stepped out into the bright sun. The field was dazzling, a perfectly cut diamond set in a huge emerald. Stunned, I took a minute to even notice the players.

But then I saw them. There they were, my players, my heroes! But real live people—Radcliff, Walker, Kuhel, Appling—with the numbers I'd studied in the newspapers stitched onto their shirts. They were taking batting practice with a graceful rhythm.

The spell was broken when someone bumped into me. I looked around the stadium, as amazing as the skyscrapers in New York. I couldn't imagine how they built this place. The ballpark was so huge and the seats went so high up, it made me dizzy. The entire population of Stockstadt would barely fill one section of seats. It was crowded outside the stadium, but thousands of seats were empty, even though it was Ladies' Day.

When I found a seat in the bleachers, I looked around and realized that here, nobody knew me, nobody knew where I was from, nobody knew that I was a Jew, and nobody cared. I was just another kid who had come to watch a ball game. For the first time since I had arrived in America, I didn't feel like an outsider.

But I worried about Greenberg, who was a Jew and a Detroit Tiger. How would he be treated by the fans? Then I thought America really must be the land of opportunity if a Jew could even play baseball here.

"Number five, Hank Greenberg, first base," the announcer's voice boomed when Greenberg stepped up to the plate in the first inning. From where I was sitting, he looked so small that I doubted he could hit a ball past the bases.

"Throw him a pork chop," one pasty-faced fan yelled to the pitcher. "He'll never touch that."

"Hey, Moses," someone else hollered. "Hey, Hebe."

"Hey, Hank," I heard one man who was sitting behind me say, "Hitler is looking for you." I froze in my seat; my stomach dropped. I wanted to turn around to see what that man looked like, but I was afraid he might see that I was Jewish, too.

I listened carefully to the crowd to see if others were saying anything like that. Most fans were cheering for him. "C'mon, Hammerin' Hank," they were saying, just as they did for all their own Chicago players. Someone called out, "Hit it to me. Right here!" "Let's get another home run. Make it twenty-six!" yelled the boy in the seat next to me, who was waving a Sox pennant. A group of Sox fans started chanting, "Twenty-six! Twenty-six! Twenty-six!"

As I watched Greenberg take his turn at bat, I remembered the newspaper story I had read a few weeks ago about how as a boy the Jewish women on his block would call him a bum or "Mrs. Greenberg's disgrace" because he wanted to play baseball rather than go to school. His immigrant parents were disappointed when he decided to become a professional baseball player.

I wondered how Hank had found the courage to go against his parents' wishes. Didn't he feel he had to do exactly what they told him to do?

The article said that Greenberg was one of the few Jewish players who didn't change his name to pass as a Christian. He refused to play on Yom Kippur, the Jewish Day of Atonement, even when the Tigers were in a pennant race. I was amazed: Hank Greenberg was proud to be a Jew and he wasn't afraid to stand up for who he was.

Being a Jew didn't seem all that important to Aunt Mildred and Uncle Jack. They didn't go to services regularly and they didn't do much to mark the Sabbath. The synagogue was more of a social circle than a religious community. But Greenberg seemed to be saying that Jews were just as American as anyone else. It made me wonder: Could I be both Jewish and American?

I was still thinking about all of this in the fifth inning, when Greenberg came up to the plate again. I felt too unsure of myself to cheer and yell. But I clenched my fists tightly as Greenberg took the first pitch, a strike, and said to myself, "Come on . . . come on, Hank. Hit one out here."

I could feel my whole body behind the next pitch, as if I were holding the bat and swinging with Hank.

He missed.

The next pitch was low, for a ball.

"Come on, Greenberg," I whispered quietly, punching

my fist into my hand as if I were wearing a mitt. "Right here. Right here."

I didn't see the next pitch, but I heard the crack of the bat. With that sound, everyone in the bleachers stood up as one, cheering and pointing at the white ball sailing against the pale blue sky.

And I stood up, too, suddenly screaming and shouting with the rest of the crowd—most of them Americans, many of them Jews like me—"Hankus Pankus! Hankus Pankus! Hankus Pankus!"

## 12

## I TOOK YOU IN

When I walked into the apartment that evening, I stopped to look around the living room. Everything was the same—yet different—from when I had left that morning. The night before, I had set out the folding table and laid Aunt Mildred's special birthday tablecloth across it. On the cloth I had placed plates, glasses, silverware, and birthday streamers—everything just right.

Now everything was still there, but it was all used and dirty The folding table in the middle of the living room was littered and piled with empty boxes, torn ribbons, and crumpled streamers. On Aunt Mildred's best china plates, dirty forks were sticking straight up in dried out, half eaten slices of chocolate cake. Wet glasses and drained soda bottles were everywhere.

"Edith," Aunt Mildred called to me as soon as I closed

the front door, "would you please clean up the living room?"

No matter where I had been, no matter what happened to me, I always returned to Aunt Mildred's chores. I went to the linen closet to put away my souvenirs—streetcar tickets and the scorecard that I had found on the ground at the game. As I shut the door, Dorothy walked by wearing a new red blouse. "After you finish," she said, "come to my room. I'll show you what I got."

My heart pounded and my face flushed. Dorothy never invited me into her bedroom. Her offer both thrilled and insulted me. Now she was nice to me, but earlier in the day I wasn't good enough to be part of her birthday celebration. Before I could think, I blurted out, "Why would you show me your gifts when you didn't even invite me to your party?"

I had never spoken up to her or Aunt Mildred, had hardly stood up for myself to anyone. I was always what Vati had asked me to be: a good girl.

Dorothy gasped. She looked surprised and hurt, raising her eyebrows and then creasing her brow.

"You know," I said, biting my lip as if I could stop the words before they rushed out of me, "I'm not just here to clean up after you and your family."

A great sense of relief came over me as I finally said what had been bothering me for so long. Then I added for punch, "I have feelings, too."

As soon as the words came out of my mouth, I regretted that I had said anything. I had broken my rules and stepped on a crack.

Aunt Mildred, listening to every word, stomped into the room in her heavy shoes. I measured her mood by the weight of her footsteps: today they were thunderous. The soda bottles on the table rattled as she approached me. The fringe on the lamp by the front door trembled.

"You're upset because you weren't invited to a sixteen-year-old's birthday party?" She was almost spitting at me. "Why would you, a fourteen-year-old girl who looks like she's ten, want to be with a bunch of boy-crazy, giggling, sixteen-year-old girls? They would probably just make fun of you and your accent and your looks."

I clasped my shaking hands behind my back to hide my fear, hung my head, and stared at the floor in shame. I must have looked like a whipped dog with its tail between its legs.

"I did you a favor!" she hissed. "Spared you teasing!" I glanced over at Dorothy. She didn't look at me, but she didn't look at Aunt Mildred either.

"And this . . . this, after all I've done. I took you into my home. I put a roof over your head. I feed you. I pay your way. And what do I get for it?

"Well, let me tell you, this may not seem like the perfect arrangement—look at me when I'm talking to you, young lady," she snapped, startling me.

Dorothy jumped, too. Then she turned her head toward me. She gave me a kind, almost sympathetic look. Had she, too, been on the receiving end of Aunt Mildred's harsh criticisms?

"Just you tell me," she demanded, "how many other German Jewish children do you see living around here?"

I felt sick.

What she said was true. In the local grammar school, there were only a few German Jewish refugee children.

"Most people here did nothing. Everyone else pretends you people don't even exist. At least I did something. In fact, I did more than most Americans.

"I took you in," she said again, standing tall, as if she were the Statue of Liberty herself.

Later, I thought about what she had said. To fully understand, I whispered her words to myself in German: *Ich hab' dich aufgenommen.*

Then I took the sentence apart, word by word. She said "I," not "we." I had always thought that Uncle Jack pushed for my living here, but she had said "I," as if this had been her decision alone. She said "took you," which is an action, an act of receiving. "In" seemed to be a statement of somehow being included, of belonging.

"I took you in." In other words, she protected me.

Nothing looked the same. I felt as if I were looking

through a shaken kaleidoscope. All the colors and shapes had changed, with the whole and its parts taking on a different appearance.

Maybe she *had* spared me from teasing by sending me away from the party. Dorothy's friends were nice to me sometimes, but I never felt that they really wanted me around. On the other hand, maybe Aunt Mildred had said she spared me from teasing as an excuse, so she didn't have to invite me to the party. Maybe *she* just didn't want me around.

I didn't know . . . just as I didn't know exactly why my parents had put me on the boat. I had seen the terrible pictures of events in Germany, but I hated that I had to find my way in America alone. I ached every minute I was on my own here.

Maybe Aunt Mildred *had* done more than most. Maybe even though she didn't look like it, she was a rescuer. My mother's letter to Uncle Jack showed how difficult it was to find a sponsor and a home. No one else had offered to "take me in," to let me live with their family, none of the Westerfelds, nor the Kahns on my mother's side who lived in South America and Palestine. It was Uncle Jack and, strangely, Aunt Mildred who had not abandoned me.

Ever since I had arrived in America, I had been trying to see how these people could be my family. Sometimes, when I felt especially alone, I wondered: Was it possible to create a family if you didn't have one? Does a family have to be related by blood? For that matter, what really is a family?

My sister had answered some of these questions for herself. She was living with people who weren't related to her, but they had become her family. When she called, every month or so, she always mentioned her "new sister," Debbie, who wasn't even a relative. But that didn't seem to matter to Betty. She'd say, "I took my sister downtown yesterday . . ." Or "I was telling my sister about my job . . ." Or "My sister and I are going out now."

With Dorothy and me, things had gotten so bad that sometimes I would jump when she said my name. So when she came up to me later that day and said, "Edith, I'd like to talk to you," I couldn't imagine what she wanted.

"Can you come in my room?" she asked, pointing toward the door.

"I don't want to see your gifts," I said.

"Not for that. Come in so we can talk in private."

Slowly I followed her into her room. She closed the door behind us, went over to the bed, sat on the pillow, and folded her legs on the white chenille bedspread. I counted four violations of Aunt Mildred's rules: No closed doors. No sitting on the pillow. No sitting on the bedspread. No shoes on the bed. Cautiously I leaned on the edge of the bed, not really sitting, just in case Aunt Mildred walked in.

I felt like I was visiting a foreign country. Often, when I went into Dorothy's room to pick up her clothes or trash, she rushed me out. "Don't do that now," she'd say. But I worried that if I didn't, Aunt Mildred would complain that I hadn't done all my chores.

I never had time to look around. Now I stared at the dozens of magazine photographs of movie stars posted on the walls. Old stuffed animals sat on her dresser. A small lamp lit up her schoolbooks on a desk in the corner. Pencils and an artist's drawing pad filled a nightstand next to her old maple bed frame. I didn't even know Dorothy could draw.

"You know——" Dorothy said as I gazed around her room. I noticed that she was looking down, fidgeting with her hands. "Edith, I guess I want to say a few things about . . about us."

"Us?" I said. I had no idea what she was talking about, since as far as I was concerned there wasn't any "us."

"Yes, us . . . you and me.

"I never had a sister or brother," she continued. "When you first came, I didn't know what to expect. I didn't know who you were or how you would fit in. I really didn't know how to treat you. And I guess I was mad that you were here."

I must have looked confused. Dorothy swallowed hard and began again. "I guess, because of all this, I haven't been very nice to you." She looked down at her hands.

"But I'm glad you said something," Dorothy continued. "It made me think about things.

"I know that my mother isn't easy to get along with," she said, after a few moments, "not for any of us—my father, you, me. A lot of times, she says hurtful things. I don't think she means to. Sometimes she just says something before she's thought it through."

I didn't say anything. I wasn't going to help her with this. A part of me wanted to give her the same treatment she had given me all these months.

"We all make mistakes. And you know my mother well enough to understand that . . . well, she doesn't ever apologize.

"So I wanted to say that I . . . I'm . . ." She stumbled, stopped, then took a deep breath.

"I'm sorry. And . . . and I want you to know that now I see that you're right." She wiped her tears with the sleeve of her new red blouse.

"Edith, I should have invited you to my birthday party."

We stared at each other for a long time, as if each wished the other would say something or make the next move. But neither of us knew what to do.

Looking closely at Dorothy's face, I felt as if I had never seen her before. Her watery eyes looked huge, deeper and darker than usual. Her face seemed softer, her curly brown hair gently framing her high cheekbones. Dorothy looked pretty to me.

Finally, I spoke.

"Show me your gifts," I said.

## 13

## CHANGE!

December 27, 1939

Dear Vati,

I'm hoping Mutti will get this letter to you. I know you are in a camp somewhere in Germany now.

I'm sitting in the Chicago Public Library. It is Christmas vacation, so I have more free time than usual. Aunt Mildred's apartment is so small that there is no place for me, so I go to the library whenever I can. I can't imagine how crowded the apartment will be when you, Mutti, and Oma Sarah come. We'll all have to go to the library!

Anyhow, ever since I went to a baseball game last summer, I have been reading every book in the library about that sport. Here, everyone talks baseball all the time, adults and kids. To be an American, I think I need to know all about the game.

It probably seems silly to you that people spend a whole afternoon watching grown men playing a game. I can hear you say, "Who has that kind of time?" But it is fun, Vati. As I told you, Onkel Jakob and I follow the Chicago White Sox, but I'm also a big fan of a Jewish player, Hank Greenberg, who plays for the Detroit Tigers and is trying to set a record with the most home runs (that means to hit the ball out of the park and score for his team).

I can't wait for April 16th, when the season begins. And I can't wait for you to get here so that I can take you to a game. Now that I've read so much about it, I'll be able to teach you the rules. Maybe we can even see Hank Greenberg hit a home run!

Love,
Tiddy

P.S. I know you don't like me to keep asking, but I hear that things are getting worse in Germany. When do you expect to have all the papers together so that you, Mutti, and Oma Sarah can come to America?

A couple of days after I wrote this letter, Mrs. Goldstein stopped by Aunt Mildred's apartment when everyone was out but me. I hadn't seen her for some time.

"Edith!" She threw her arms around me as soon as I opened the door. No one ever hugged me except Mrs.

Goldstein. The snow that dusted her wool coat refreshed my face and her perfume smelled sweet. "I figured you'd be home during the day since it's Christmas vacation." She stepped into the hallway entrance and took a long hard look at me from head to toe. "It's been a while."

"Come in," I said. She stomped her wet boots, took off her coat, and placed it carefully on the cane chair with a hole in the seat. I went into the living room, and she followed me to the couch.

"You look good, Edith," she said. "How do you feel?"

"Pretty good," I said, looking down, avoiding her eyes. I knew what Mrs. Goldstein was asking. It was the same thing she had asked me each time she visited. I knew she was worried about me.

I was the smallest girl in my class, and the only one who had not yet gotten her period. I had confessed to Mrs. Goldstein on her last visit months ago that I hated going to physical education class. There I was reminded, not once but twice a day, that I was as out of place now as when I arrived as a seventh grader and was put in a first-grade classroom. Then I looked like an adult among children; now I looked like a child among adults.

Before and after PE, when I had to change my clothes, I tried to hide behind my locker door. Some days, I wore a loose bra that Dorothy had thrown away to pretend I was like the other ninth-grade girls.

"Flat as an ironing board," one girl always said when I

took off my blouse. She had a sharp Chicago accent and the "a" in "flat" sounded long and strange to me.

"Are there any mountains in Germany?" another girl would ask.

"Nope, not even a baby hill!" And they would laugh as my face burned with embarrassment.

Every day, I hoped that I would get my period. Every month, I was disappointed when I didn't. If I did get it, I didn't know what I would do. I had noticed that none of the American girls in my PE class wore cotton rags like the ones Mutti had sent with me.

"Any change?" Mrs. Goldstein asked, arching her dark eyebrows.

"No." I looked out the window, avoiding her.

"It's okay, Edith." She patted my knee. "You know, sometimes this happens to girls who have great emotional upset. They stop growing for a while. I talked to a doctor and he recommended that you get hormone treatments. That would get you growing . . . and fast. For some girls, I think the changes practically happen overnight. Would you be willing to try this?"

"Yes," I said, without giving it a second thought. Anything to stop the teasing. Anything to fit in with my classmates.

Mrs. Goldstein and I decided to wait a few more months before making the appointment with the doctor. Nothing had changed by the time spring came, and she began taking me to the doctor for hormone shots right around the time baseball season began.

Now, even more than last season, I followed Hammerin' Hank's every move. Whenever the Tigers played the White Sox, I listened to the game on the radio. Every day, I couldn't wait to read news stories and box scores in the *Chicago Daily News*. Sometimes, on the train ride downtown to the doctor, I would bring the newspaper stories about Hank Greenberg and tell Mrs. Goldstein about him.

"You know, he's six feet, three and a half inches and he weighs two hundred ten pounds," I said. "That's how he hits all those homers."

"You are really smitten with Hank," Mrs. Goldstein gently teased me.

"Smitten?" I asked. "What does that mean?"

"Love struck." I could feel myself blushing as Mrs. Goldstein grinned.

"No . . . just a big fan," I said.

On the shelf in the linen closet, I kept my brown Hank Greenberg envelope containing the scorecard from the day I had seen him play, along with a growing pile of newspaper articles I began clipping that spring. Hankus Pankus led the league in home runs, runs batted in, and doubles that summer and helped the Detroit Tigers win the pennant that fall. Greenberg became the first player to win the American League Most Valuable Player at two different positions. My overstuffed envelope was ripping apart by the end of the 1940 season.

I simply couldn't get enough of Hammerin' Hank. I knew all sorts of details about his life. Where he lived. What car he drove. Who he was dating. I even knew his license plate number—U99.

Maybe I was "smitten." Even Dorothy said one day while she watched me clip articles about Hank, "You act like Hank Greenberg is Clark Gable."

As the Tigers fell to the Cincinnati Reds in the 1940 World Series, the sports columnists started writing about how different the game would be next year. The United States wasn't at war yet, but President Roosevelt had created a military draft, registering men between the ages of twenty-one and thirty. If war came, even baseball players might be drafted.

But they wouldn't draft a big star like Hammerin' Hank—at least, I didn't *think* they would. Still, I was relieved when the draft board doctors pronounced Greenberg ineligible for the Army because he had "flat feet." Then some newspaper writers began to complain that Greenberg was getting special treatment. They insisted that he be examined again. Soon, a different doctor said Hank was fit enough to serve.

When I read the news, I slammed my scissors on the dining room table. This article I would not clip! If I didn't save it, maybe it wouldn't be true. How could they do this to me? And to all the other fans and even the game of baseball? Just two years earlier, Greenberg had almost broken Babe Ruth's record of sixty homers in one season. I dreamed of rooting for Hammerin' Hank the season he would hit sixty-one. Imagine! A Jew shattering the most important record in all of baseball. Now, if he had to serve overseas, he would lose his chance to beat the Babe.

But he would have a chance to stop the Nazis. Maybe he could save my family or even help my parents come to America.

Still, I didn't want to give him up. Hank was like a caring uncle or big brother. Whenever the girls in the locker room called me an anti-Jewish name, I reminded myself that Hank has been through this.

Now, I asked myself, how will I get through next summer without him? Even worse, what if he got hurt? Or what if he . . . ? I couldn't even let myself think of anything worse.

I wiped my eyes and put away the scissors. There must be something I could do to keep him safe. For weeks, I wished I had a rabbit's foot or some lucky charm to protect him.

Then I figured out the perfect way to keep Hank close to me. I could wear my mother's Jewish star. But I'd have to ask Dorothy if I could have it. Ever since she had apologized about her birthday party, things had been different between us. We still weren't close—but it felt like there was a silent understanding between us—like we both were on the same team.

One afternoon when she was doing homework in her bedroom, I stood outside her door, working up the nerve to ask. Knock, I told myself. She doesn't ever wear the necklace. Come on, knock. She won't even miss it. Finally, I heard my knuckles rap softly on the door.

"Come in," Dorothy called.

I stepped in and closed the door behind me.

"Did you . . . do you . . ."

Dorothy was sitting at the desk, her world history book open in front of her, writing in a school notebook. "What is it?" she asked, without looking up.

"Do . . . do you still have my mother's Star of David?"

"Yeah," she said, erasing something she had just written.

"I was wondering . . . could I wear it for a while?"

Dorothy stopped erasing and looked at me. She went straight to her top dresser drawer and found the small, shiny star and chain. "Sure," she said. "Go ahead and wear it."

"Thank you!" I was thrilled to have it. I ran to the hall mirror, clasped the delicate gold chain behind my neck, and remembered as I put it on the day my mother had taken it off for good. "It's no longer safe to wear this in Germany," she had said, as she removed it from her neck. I tucked the necklace under my blouse and felt the Star of David near my heart.

One day during Christmas vacation, in late 1940, I awakened and knew, even before I sat up, that things felt different. I had noticed some small changes over the last few months, but now, suddenly, I knew I wasn't the same person I had been the day before. Moving around on the couch, I felt as if I took up more space against the pillows. I had grown taller and curvier almost overnight. Finally, I was growing breasts! But I felt as if I were in someone else's body, like Alice after she swallowed the drink on the table in *Alice's Adventures in Wonderland*.

When I went back to high school on the first Monday after Christmas vacation, I was nervous about how those girls in my PE class who had been teasing me for years would treat me now that I had "mountains," or at least "hills." I still wore the hand-me-down bra from Dorothy, but I was much closer to filling it out. When I had to get undressed in class, I didn't hide behind the locker. I decided to take my clothes off in front of everyone. When they saw my new body, I hoped the teasing would stop, once and for all.

I felt the eyes of several girls upon me. The ones who

always mocked me stood in a line, staring so hard I thought they would burn a hole in me. My heart pounded and blood rushed in my ears, but I was determined to show them that I was just like them.

I kept my eyes on my buttons. My hands shook as I undid each one on the front of my blouse. Then I slipped my arms out of the sleeves.

Nobody said a word.

Except the PE teacher. "Don't just stand there, girls," Mrs. Murray called out as she walked past the gawkers. "Change! Right now!"

In spring, about a month after the 1941 baseball season began, the bad news came. The *Sporting News* reported that in his farewell game, Hank Greenberg hit two home runs to help the Tigers beat the Yankees. The next morning, the paper said, baseball's highest-paid player, the "Jewish Babe Ruth," and three hundred other draftees would be inducted into the United States Army in an old corset factory in Detroit.

"If there's any last message to be given to the public," Hammerin' Hank told the crowd, "let it be that I'm going to be a good soldier."

It was a long, sad season without Hank. I didn't get to any of the White Sox games that summer. When the Detroit Tigers came to town, I didn't even listen to the games. Instead, I rubbed my Star of David between my thumb and finger extra times and thought of Hank.

Miraculously, in early December, President Roosevelt announced that he was honorably discharging all men over twenty-eight years of age. Hank Greenberg was thirty. Hankus Pankus would be back in the Detroit Tigers' lineup for the 1942 season! As I read the story, a popular song that the radio played whenever Hank hit a home run popped into my head, "Goodbye, Mr. Ball, Goodbye." I kissed my gold star, sure that it had worked its magic.

Then, only a few days later—on Sunday, December 7, 1941—everything changed. Japan attacked the United States by bombing Pearl Harbor. The Americans soon declared war on Japan and, three days later, on Italy and Germany. What did this mean?

Was this good or bad news for my family? Now they were trapped in Germany. Would the Americans bomb Stockstadt? Would my parents survive? Would they ever get out?

"We are in trouble," Hank Greenberg told the newspapers. "There is only one thing for me to do—return to the service. This doubtless means I am finished with baseball and it would be silly for me to say I do not leave it without a pang. But all of us are confronted with a terrible task— the defense of our country and the fight for our lives."

It certainly felt like the fight for *my* family's life.

Around the time Hammerin' Hank announced that he

was returning to duty, I received an official letter from the Department of Immigration:

*December 15, 1941*
*Miss Westerfeld:*

*Under the United States statutes contained within Title 50, Chapter 3 of the U.S. Code, you have been identified as an enemy alien. This term applies only to persons fourteen years of age or older who are within the United States and not actually naturalized. Under this provision, all "natives, citizens, denizens or subjects" of any foreign nation or government with which the United States is at war "are liable to be apprehended, restrained, secured and removed as alien enemies."*

*By January 31, 1942, you must report to your local post office for a certificate of registration. You will be fingerprinted and photographed. You will be required to carry your photo-bearing "enemy alien registration card," the AR-3, at all times and you will be restricted in your travels. When you report to the post office, you must surrender your hand cameras, short-wave radio receiving sets, and radio transmitters.*

*The government has the power to detain and to arrest any enemy alien who does not cooperate with this law or anyone who endangers the peace and good order of the United States.*

*The Department of Immigration*

I read the letter twice, struggling to understand it. Then I did what I always did when I got scared or angry: I asked myself what Hank Greenberg would think.

But this, I knew, would never happen to him. Hank Greenberg was Jewish like me, but he was an American, a baseball hero, an honorable soldier. And me—I was an enemy alien.

## 14

## LABELED

An enemy alien. Now I would have to register with the U.S. government. Years ago in Germany, my family had had to register as Jews. What did this new registration mean?

I tried to postpone going to register, but Uncle Jack reminded me every day. "Edith, you have a date with the postmaster," he said. Finally, when he figured I might not go on my own, he offered to take me on the first Wednesday of my school's holiday break.

We were just about to leave for the post office when Betty called. "You realize what all this means, right?"

"Sort of," I said. Uncle Jack said that because America had declared war on Germany and I was a citizen of the enemy's country, the government would be watching me.

"Well, I'm afraid things are going to change for us," Betty said.

"But how?"

"For one thing, I can't come see you this weekend."

"Why not?" I wasn't surprised to hear this. Betty only came to visit me every few months, and she often canceled for one reason or another. I knew that it was a long trip; she had to transfer—trains and streetcars—to get here. But I always felt disappointed when she couldn't make it. And I had begun to suspect that she didn't want to come too often. Now that we had separate lives, it was difficult to be in each other's company. Maybe we reminded each other of all that was lost from our childhoods.

But not seeing each other at all was worse. I was afraid I would be completely cut off from any connection to the past.

"You live more than twenty miles away, Edith," Betty said. "We're enemy aliens, so we can't travel that far without a pass. It will take more than a few days to get police permission."

"But I really want to see you. Can't you come anyway?" I knew my voice sounded like a complaint, but I couldn't help myself.

"Edith!" she said sharply. "You don't want me to get arrested and put in a camp, do you?"

"No, no!" That was the last thing I wanted. The word "camp" seemed to mean so many things. I thought it best for us to avoid camps completely.

Then a new worry struck me. Maybe we shouldn't even be talking on the phone.

"Do you think they're bugging us, Betty?" I asked. I'd seen a movie about the FBI keeping track of people by listening in on their phone conversations.

"I don't know, Edith. But the law is that we can't even be out after eight at night." Betty was speaking in a low voice now, almost whispering. "I talked to a teacher at school and he said that I shouldn't speak any German; I shouldn't even say where I'm from."

"It feels strange to say this," I said, "but I'm glad the United States is fighting Germany."

"Yeah, me, too," Betty said. "One thing is for sure, Germany isn't good for us."

"Us? Who do you mean by 'us'?"

"Us as Jews and us as Americans."

Well, if the FBI was listening, I figured they wouldn't mind hearing this.

"But I'm scared for Mutti and Vati," I said, "and Oma Sarah and Mina."

I heard Betty swallow hard.

"Me, too," she whispered. "Me, too."

At the crowded post office, Uncle Jack and I waited in line to see the clerk behind the counter, who was busy selling people sheets of postage stamps for Christmas cards and weighing large boxes of holiday gifts to mail. I couldn't help remembering the time I had waited in line all day with my father at the American consulate back in Frankfurt.

"Good afternoon," Uncle Jack said to the clerk after a twenty-minute wait. "My niece needs to fill out forms for the AR-3."

"What about you?" he asked sharply, hearing Uncle Jack's accent. My heart pounded; the clerk's harsh manner and crisp uniform reminded me of the Nazis. I felt my mother's Star of David cold against my skin.

"I have my papers." Uncle Jack sounded insulted.

"Just one, then?" The clerk eyed him.

"Yes," Uncle Jack said with an edge to his voice. "Just one."

The clerk searched through brown file folders to get out the forms, then turned to me and asked, "Do you have a hand camera, short-wave radio receiving set, or radio transmitter?"

"Well . . ." I glanced up at Uncle Jack, trying to figure out whether I should tell the clerk about the camera.

"Do you?" He leaned forward and stared hard at me.

"Sort of," I said, frightened.

"What do you mean, 'sort of'? What do you have?" The man looked angry now, not just suspicious.

Uncle Jack cut in. "She doesn't own a camera. Once in a while I lend her my old Leica."

"You must turn that over to us within a week," the clerk said, still glaring at me.

"But it's not her camera." Uncle Jack gripped the counter tightly. "It's mine."

"Doesn't matter who owns it," the clerk said flatly. "If she uses it, it must be turned over to us."

"You know," Uncle Jack leaned over the counter and said quietly, "she's not exactly who you are looking for. She's a sixteen-year-old girl who uses her uncle's camera to take pictures for school projects."

"Doesn't matter." The clerk shoved the papers toward me. "She's an enemy alien. She has the use of a camera."

He pointed toward a long counter under the back window. "Go over there to fill out these forms," he said loudly. As we turned away, he called out even louder so that everyone in the post office could hear: "That camera must be turned in within a week!"

My cheeks burned with shame. It was as if he had just announced proof that I was a spy.

We joined about ten people, mostly adults, who were all filling out the same forms. Curious to see whom the government was watching, I looked down the line. Several people looked Japanese or Chinese and weren't speaking English. They huddled with friends or relatives who were translating the forms for them. The man next to Uncle Jack looked European. When Uncle Jack apologized for accidentally bumping the man's elbow, he answered, *"Mi scusi! Mi scusi! No, no, non è un problema."*

To my right, next to the wall, a brown-haired boy about my age stood with his back to me as he busily worked over the forms. His head was bent so low that all I could see was his shaggy hair sticking out along the collar of his jacket.

I watched him closely while I waited for Uncle Jack to read over the forms. As I stared, the boy raised his head, his eyes darting around the room. Then he looked straight at me, just long enough so that I was sure he saw me.

My stomach dropped. It was Julius. He looked away quickly, as if he didn't know me.

While Uncle Jack and I filled out the forms, I kept glancing at Julius. His face was thinner, but there was no mistaking his blue eyes. Every so often, he looked around the room guardedly, but never in my direction. He hunched over the papers as if he didn't want anyone to see that he was filling out AR-3 forms. Maybe he had come to our local post office so he wouldn't see anyone he knew.

On the cold walk back to Aunt Mildred's apartment, Uncle Jack was quiet. I knew he felt uncomfortable that the government had put me through all this.

"I'm sorry about your camera," I said, noticing that the day had turned gray and now looked like snow. "It's hard to give up something that you brought over from Germany."

"Yes, that's too bad," he said. "But it's not your fault."

"Maybe," I said, "I shouldn't have said anything about it."

"You did the right thing," he assured me. "But I don't like what America is doing."

I didn't either, and the camera was the least of it. I was worried about how far this would go.

Being identified as an alien was painful for me, but I thought it must be especially hard on Julius, who was so determined to be an American. I wondered what he wrote in the box that asked for his name: Julius or Jerry?

But no matter what he called himself, America had its own label, its own classification for Julius and me: other.

## 15

## WHAT DID YOU EXPECT?

Baseball's spring training opened in early 1942. Sports-writers tried to capture the excitement of the new season, but they also filled their columns with news about players who were going off to war, like the Boston Red Sox slugger Ted Williams and the Cleveland Indians pitcher Bob Feller.

Those baseball stars meant nothing to me. I scoured every section of the newspaper for only one name: Hank Greenberg. Finally, one day, I found a small story buried in the sports pages: "Sgt Greenberg Trains Near Tigers." It said that Hank was a sergeant in the Air Force at MacDill Field in Tampa, Florida, "just around the corner"—about thirty miles—from Lakeland, the Tigers' spring training camp.

Even without Hank, I still cared about baseball and

my South Side Chicago team. Opening day for the White Sox was an unusually warm, breezy Tuesday in the middle of April, holding all the promise of summer ahead. I couldn't wait for school to end, though I knew Aunt Mildred would add extra chores to my list: washing windows, wiping the baseboards, scrubbing between the tiles in the bathroom.

I had my own plans for this summer. If I had any free time, I hoped to work for pay, so that I could send more money to my parents. I already knew it wouldn't be easy to get a job. Anywhere I might apply—the soda shop, the five-and-dime store, the library—someone would ask for my papers. Then I would have to show my AR-3 card. Who would hire an enemy alien?

But on that April day after school, I wasn't thinking about being an alien. I was taking the long way to Aunt Mildred's, walking slowly along the lake and spending a few extra minutes in the beautiful weather. When I get to the apartment, I thought, I'll listen to the last inning of the White Sox versus the St. Louis Browns while I do my chores—that is, if Aunt Mildred isn't stuck to the radio, listening to her daily soap operas.

I entered the stuffy apartment and shuffled through the mail on the hallway table. In the pile was an airmail letter to me, postmarked from Switzerland, with no return address. Strange, I thought. I recognized Mina's handwriting on the envelope, but what was she doing in Switzerland? For some reason, my hand shook as I opened the envelope. The letter was dated two months earlier, in February.

*Dearest Tiddy,*

*This is the letter I hoped I would never write. I have to make sure you get it. My friend, who is going to Switzerland, will mail it to you from there, since the German government is censoring the mail that leaves the country now.*

*I wish I could sit down and talk to you and not send this letter. Oh! I wish we were together!*

*With great sadness, I must tell you that both of your parents and your grandmother have died in concentration camps. I only learned the news last week.*

*Tiddy, you should know that your mother cried every day after you left. She refused to give away any of your things—especially your blue bike. That was how she held on to you. Your father, too. He loved you very much.*

*It is not easy to live here now, Tiddy, without my dear Westerfelds. I am thankful that you didn't see the terrible things that went on here. I'm glad that you are living in freedom in America.*

*For days, I have been writing this letter in my head, trying to think of what to say. How will we go on? Here's what I know: they died, but you must live. Me, too.*

*To honor their memory, Tiddy, we must live.*
*Please write to me, I miss you so.*

*Love,*
*Mina*

A strange, loud noise startled me—a moan that sounded like an injured animal's cry. It took me a moment to realize that it had come from my own throat. I felt like I had been punched in the stomach—doubled over from the blow, mouth wide open, trying to breathe.

Gasping for air, I sat down on the broken cane chair in the entrance. I couldn't catch my breath. *Atme.* I tried to concentrate on just taking air into my lungs and then letting it out. *Atme.* Several minutes passed, I think. Maybe even half an hour. I couldn't tell.

From my seat I could see that Aunt Mildred was settled in her stuffed maroon chair. Her shiny red fingernails stroked its worn upholstery as she leaned toward the console radio, listening to *My Sister Ruth*, one of her favorite radio dramas. I stared at her for a long time as I worked to breathe.

Then I stood up. Slowly, shakily, I took a few steps into the living room.

When Aunt Mildred saw me, she frowned and turned down the volume slightly.

"What is it?" She seemed irritated that I had interrupted her.

When I didn't answer, she raised her voice over the chatter of the radio. "What's the matter with you?" she snapped.

"My parents," I said. We hadn't spoken of them in months. Aunt Mildred had never shown much interest, even when they wrote to me.

"Well? What about them?" she asked sharply.

"They're . . . they've been . . ." Now I was sobbing again, unable to speak. Somehow, it seemed that if I said the word, the news would become real. But I couldn't stay silent forever.

"They're . . . they're . . . dead. Dead."

Aunt Mildred stared at me for a moment. Then she said, "What did you expect?" Her voice was barely above a whisper. "What did you expect?"

That evening, Uncle Jack approached me when I was curled in the corner of the living room couch.

"Edith? Talk to me." He sat down next to me. "Edith, you know I tried to help. I did what I could to get your parents out of Germany. But it was so difficult from this end. There just wasn't much I could do. I tried to raise money through the synagogue. I raised some, but not enough. And now . . ." He paused, his eyes filling with tears. "Now it's too late.

"You know, he was my brother." Uncle Jack lifted his

glasses and wiped his tears with the same broad fingers as my father. "I'm suffering, too, Edith."

Uncle Jack hadn't seen Vati in so many years, I thought he wouldn't really feel the loss. I looked hard at him. His face looked the way my parents' had when they said good-bye to me at the dock—gray and defeated.

The next evening, Dorothy invited me into her room.

I shook my head in silence. It was too much effort even to say no, never mind trying to get up off the couch.

"Just for a minute, Edith," she said. Aunt Mildred glanced up from the radio and gave me a look, telling me to do as Dorothy asked. I followed her into her room.

"I'm so sorry," Dorothy said as she sat down on her bed. She patted the bedspread, inviting me to sit, but I stood by the door with my arms folded across my chest.

"I can't imagine how hard this is for you," Dorothy said. "I . . . I was praying it wouldn't turn out like this."

I felt the points of the gold star prick my chest. I had thought it would protect Hank. Now I knew I couldn't keep anyone safe. There was no reason to wear the star anymore. I reached behind my head, undid the clasp, and handed the necklace to Dorothy.

"Wasn't this your mother's?" She looked closely at the chain and star in her hand.

I nodded.

"Then I think you should keep it," Dorothy said. She

came up behind me, put the chain around my neck, and hooked the clasp. Now the Jewish star had nothing to do with Hank; it was all I had left of my mother. Dorothy had never worn it, but I would never take it off.

When I turned around to say thank you, she gave me an awkward hug. I slipped away from her and into the bathroom, shutting the door with my shoulder and slumping down on the floor.

It was a long time before I came out, but no one knocked. Lost in my own thoughts, I didn't even hear the telephone ring later that evening, but I did hear Aunt Mildred's shrill call.

"Eee-*dith!*" I jumped as she dropped the black receiver on the hallway table. I knew it was Betty; no one else ever called me, except Mrs. Goldstein, and she wouldn't call at night.

I didn't want to talk to anyone, even my sister. I slowly walked to the table and picked up the telephone.

"Hello?"

"*Guten Abend, Tiddy?*"

"I—*ja?*" I stumbled, trying to come up with "yes" in the right language. I was startled to hear her speak German and to call me by my old German nickname.

"*Ich nehme an, du hast einen Brief von Mina bekommen.* I suppose you got a letter from Mina."

"Yes," I said, with a catch in my throat.

"*Wie geht's dir, Tiddy?* How are you, Tiddy?"

I couldn't speak.

"I mean, I know how hard this is." Betty was nineteen now, although she still lived with her foster family. "I know you were too young to understand what was happening in Germany. Maybe even too young to see what was going on around you."

I said nothing as Betty spoke. "Mutti and Vati didn't think this would happen," she continued. "They saw that things were bad, but they never thought it would turn out like this. They did the best they could by sending us to America. Do you understand that? *Verstehst du das?*"

"I can't talk now." I cut her off. Hearing her German brought on a new rush of pain. I had to stop it.

"Tiddy, please," Betty said. I could hear that she was crying. "Maybe we can talk in a few days. Will you call me?"

"Yes, maybe," I said. "Maybe in a few days." But I knew I wouldn't call. She couldn't comfort me. No one could.

The telephone receiver felt heavy in my hand. As I placed it on its cradle, a picture came into my mind: the little broken boy who wanted to go to the zoo.

Back then, on the *Deutschland*, the rest of us were living in the hope that our parents would soon join us. They had told us this was only a temporary separation, and we believed them. Soon we would be with our families again, in America.

But the broken boy knew all along. He had understood then what we could not, what I was just now beginning to see: that we were, each of us, alone.

## 16

## WE MUST LIVE

In the weeks that followed, I felt I didn't know who I was or how I might behave, from day to day, even minute to minute. Everything ached. I was tired all the time.

My head spun with my parents' promises. "I think we're close now." "We'll be together soon." "See you in America." Words I'd heard just before I had left. Words they had repeated in every letter.

Mutti and Vati had not come and now they never would. They'd never be with me again. I was angry, especially at Vati. He was the one who had been trying to keep those promises. But I was even angrier at myself. I kept hearing Vati's last request at the dock: "Do what you can from America. Send money for the passage." I had worked hard, saving almost every penny I got in my German Immigration Fund. Every six months, I had sent my savings to Mutti. But in all the years I had been here in America, I had only been able to send them a small part of the fare for just a single passenger. Not nearly enough. Maybe Vati had failed me, but I had failed him, too.

I couldn't enjoy anything. Just like when I had come over on the boat years ago, I wasn't hungry and, when I did eat, nothing had any taste—even ice cream. Sorrow was always with me. And when I experienced things that had brought me pleasure in the past—a warm day, a walk, a meal with braided bread, anything that I might have shared with my parents—I was overwhelmed with grief.

Lake Michigan especially haunted me. It brought back memories of the summer I was seven years old, when Vati taught me to swim in the Rhein River. He would paddle in a little rowboat, or sometimes just drift in the current, as I swam alongside. He never let me get too far from him.

Many evenings, especially when he had had a bad day, he would go and sit on the banks of the Rhein as the sun was setting. For hours, he would watch the barges come down the river. When he returned home, he'd tell me, "*Das Wasser beruhigi mich immer, Tiddy*. The water always calms me, Tiddy."

I thought of going to sit by the water, but I couldn't. It would only remind me of what was gone, especially Vati.

But, even at a distance, I couldn't help but notice the lake's changing colors. When it was green, it brought me back to the Rhein River and my German childhood. When it was gray, it became a mirror of my mourning. When it was blue, I sensed the wall dividing my parents from me.

Once the water held the possibility of reunion. Now it separated the present from the past, the living from the dead.

Often I dreamed about my parents. In my dreams, I would spot the backs of their heads—Mutti's knotted brown bun next to the white of Vati's bald spot. I wished they would turn around so that I could see them . . . just one more time.

Surviving felt like its own punishment. What had I done to deserve this? How could I live if my parents weren't *somewhere* in this world?

I wanted some way to keep them with me every moment. So one day, I tore a small hole in the sleeve of the smocked white blouse my mother had made for me just before I had left. It was the only piece of clothing from Germany that Aunt Mildred hadn't thrown out. I remembered that my mother had torn her dress when her older brother, my uncle Ludwig, died.

"Why did you do that?" I asked Mutti at the time.

"Jews tear their clothing to show that their being has been ripped by loss," she had told me. She wore that torn dress for a month.

Even though it was several sizes too small, I decided to wear my torn German top every day, always under a sweater so that Aunt Mildred wouldn't see it. But the blouse was so snug that I could hardly breathe.

One Saturday in late spring, while walking back to Aunt Mildred's after picking up milk at the grocery store, I watched a long black sedan pull up in front of a small redbrick home, just one block from the apartment. Curious to find out what was going on, I stopped and watched.

In the living room window of the house hung a white flag with a blue star sewn in the middle. People displayed these "blue star" banners to show that a family member was serving in the U.S. military and that they hoped for a safe return.

As I watched, two officers in crisp, formal Army uniforms slowly climbed out of the car. Their shiny patent leather shoes clicked on the sidewalk, and then on the four cement steps, as they walked up to the door. Standing on the landing, they looked at each other knowingly. Then, one man knocked firmly three times.

An older woman wearing a white apron opened the door.

"No! No! No!" she shrieked when she saw the two Army uniforms. She slammed the door on the men before they could say a word. Her crying and howling spilled out into the street, even though the windows were closed.

I turned away and ran. Still, even when I was far away from her house, that woman's cries echoed in my mind. All week long, just before I fell asleep, I heard her howling.

The following Saturday, while walking back from the

drugstore where I had bought some cosmetic creams for Aunt Mildred, I noticed that blue or gold star flags hung in house after house, building after building, up and down the block.

I passed the redbrick house where the black sedan had stopped. A gold star banner now hung in the window, replacing the blue star flag. That meant her son had been killed.

I heard the woman's terrible cries again. They grew louder and louder. I slowed down and stared, trying to figure out what I was hearing. I didn't know, but I wanted to get away.

"Stop!" I pleaded out loud as I ran down the street. She couldn't possibly hear me now.

"Stop!" I covered my ears.

Now stars flashed before my eyes: blue and gold stars, more than there could be in all the windows in Chicago. I could barely see the sidewalk as I ran to Aunt Mildred's. Everywhere I looked, I saw more stars.

I couldn't breathe. My heart pounded fast and hard. My head spun and sweat soaked my blouse.

*Das Wasser,* my father's voice came to me. *Das Wasser beruhigt mich immer, Tiddy,* he was saying. The water always calms me.

*Ja, das Wasser,* I said, answering Vati.

My father's voice comforted me, just as the water calmed him. Over and over again, I heard him say, *Das*

*Wasser.* Soon I was climbing the stairs to Aunt Mildred's apartment, trying to walk steadily and breathe evenly.

No one was in the apartment. I quickly took off my sweater, pants, and torn smocked blouse, put on old cleaning clothes, and eagerly started Aunt Mildred's chores. Usually I hated waxing the kitchen floor on my hands and knees, but today it didn't bother me, as long as I didn't see stars and hear moans. They faded for a while, but they didn't go away. Maybe, I thought, when I finish my chores, I'll do what Vati suggested and sit on the beach at Lake Michigan. Maybe the water would calm me.

After changing Aunt Mildred's bedsheets, the last chore on my list, I went to the linen closet for fresh clothes. By now, what I was wearing reeked of vinegar, bleach, and sweat. When I opened the closet door, I saw my old doll Arno leaning against the back wall of the shelf. I grabbed him and stuffed him in my purse. Then I changed right there, putting on a fresh pair of slacks and pulling the torn smocked blouse Mutti had made me over my head. Some of the stitching in the side seam popped. I wore it anyway. I didn't even put anything over it.

It was nearly six o'clock by the time I reached the beach, the end of a warm, overcast day that felt like rain. A few people were walking along the shore. I took off my shoes and socks; the sand felt cold. Grains of sand seeped around my toes—something I hadn't felt since Germany.

Whitecaps edged the gray-blue waves, and the water smelled of fish and seaweed, just like the Rhein.

"No!" I heard the woman wailing again as I sat down on the last of the dry sand by the water. "No!"

Seagulls circled above me, their high-pitched calls mixing with the woman's shrieks. Taking a deep breath, I watched the gulls dance in the air and dive for fish, just like the seagulls that had hovered over the *Deutschland*.

"I wish I could be a seagull," Gertie had said one afternoon as we stood on the deck watching the birds. "Free to go where I please."

"Where would you go?" I asked.

"Home."

"Me, too," I had said softly. "Me, too."

I stared as hard as I could, as far as I could see, looking east, at the horizon, toward home. Sitting at the beach seemed like the closest I could get to my parents.

I began to cry, quietly at first. I pulled out Arno from my purse, burying my nose in his stuffed body, inhaling the smell of home. As I did, something deep in me seemed to crack and break. For a long time, I moaned, gasped, and worked just to breathe. Every so often, the screams came again. I wasn't sure what was real and what was in my mind.

Finally, when I caught my breath, I heard voices mur-

muring. Mutti, Vati, Mina, Oma Sarah, all talking to me at the same time. I could only make out bits of words, accents, the rhythm of speech.

*Für uns Juden ist das Leben das höchste Gut* was the only complete sentence I caught. I had heard that line before, but who said it? I tried to remember. Was it Vati? It sounded like something he would say, but the voice I heard wasn't his.

*Für uns Juden ist das Leben das höchste Gut.*

Was that Rabbi Rubinstein, back home in Germany? He had said in Hebrew class one day, "We Jews value life above all else." Then I remembered the rest of what he had said. "There is a Jewish saying: 'He who acts to save a single life acts to save the entire world.' "

Could I believe that? Could the gold star mother whose son had been killed think that was true?

Blue and gold star banners hung in windows all over the South Side of Chicago, and I was certain in neighborhoods everywhere, all over the country. So many flags, for millions of American servicemen and servicewomen.

Each of those banners, I realized, blue or gold, told the whole world about those families and what they had sacrificed. American soldiers were fighting to stop Hitler, fighting so no more Westerfelds would be murdered. And not one of them even knew my family.

I had read in the newspaper that Hank Greenberg's

mother had a blue star hanging in her window. I wished I could do something. Something for Mrs. Greenberg . . . and something for this gold star mother.

I imagined myself walking up the four cement steps to her redbrick bungalow and knocking. When she'd hear someone at the door, at first, she'd panic. Then, she'd remember—the worst already had happened.

What would I say to her?

"My name is Edith Westerfeld. I came to this country from Germany when I was twelve, all by myself. My parents couldn't come with me. I've stayed with an aunt and uncle in an apartment around the corner from you. But I've lived for the day my parents would come to America."

Then I would tell her what happened—except I couldn't stand to think of what happened.

"Just a few months ago, I found out . . ."

I couldn't say it.

"I just learned . . ."

I couldn't put the truth in words.

"I know now . . ."

Just seven words. But now, they completely defined me.

"Mutti and Vati died in concentration camps."

Seven words. I heard them again. "Mutti and Vati died in concentration camps."

Slowly taking the words in, I swallowed hard and held

Arno close to my heart. For the first time, I realized I was looking at my own gold stars.

The Nazis had ruined so many lives—in Germany, in America, all over the globe. They had destroyed this mother's world and my own. I struggled to think of what I could say to her.

"I know your son was killed in the war. Thank you for what you've given your country . . . and my homeland.

"You and I, both of us, have lost so much."

Here, on the beach, the light was fading into a grayish green darkness—the color of German *Pfefferminz* tea. The line of the horizon was hard to see.

I remembered the broken boy on the boat. When we entered New York Harbor, on that cold bright morning in 1938, he couldn't see what was right in front of him: the magnificence of the Statue of Liberty, the angle of the sun's rays, the break of dawn over the ocean.

But I had seen it all and I remembered everything. In my mind I returned to that morning, to watch first how the great statue's face had caught the early pink light of day. Then I remembered how the skyline of New York City had glowed.

A few minutes passed, and I could no longer make out the waves. But I could hear them, rhythmically rolling and slapping the shore. The sun was setting behind me, and the trees in the distance were black against the darkening gray sky. It was twilight, that confusing in-between time.

What was it now, I wondered, night or day? An ending or a beginning?

Maybe it was both.

And to find out, I knew I must live.

## AFTERWORD

What is left when a child has everything taken away—home, family, language, loyalties, identity? Only a story remains.

Until recently, most Americans knew nothing of the role the United States played in saving European Jewish children from the Nazis. In 2000, after seeing a documentary about England's Kindertransport program—which saved ten thousand European children—two American women, Iris Posner and Lenore Moskowitz, became curious about their country's part in rescuing the youngest victims of Nazi persecution. As they began their research, they discovered a forgotten American rescue operation organized by Lutherans, Quakers, and Jews that took place from 1934 to 1945. Children ranging in age from fourteen months to sixteen years entered the United States in small groups, averaging about a dozen a month, roughly one hundred a year. Ultimately, these American volunteers saved twelve hundred children.

Although these children were legal immigrants, they

were not always greeted warmly in their new homeland, as this was a time of restrictive American immigration policies and widespread anti-Semitism. The children were sent to live in cities across the country, and often were forced to assimilate quickly to American culture. Consequently, most of them never felt a sense of cohesiveness as a group. Posner, the founder of the One Thousand Children foundation, believes that the circumstances of their journey and subsequent assimilation "resulted in the lack of a collective identity" among the children.

About two hundred fifty of the eight hundred surviving "children"—now in their seventies or eighties—came to the first reunion for the One Thousand Children held in Chicago in 2002. Most, like my mother, had no idea of how they had been brought to America. No one knew they had been part of a larger rescue effort. Posner told the group, "You will not find these stories in history books."

Stories of other immigrant children often aren't featured in history books either. For many reasons—war, famine, political persecution, economic hardship, natural disasters—children have been painfully separated from their parents and forced to find a new life. These drastic uprootings cast these young people adrift, even as they are rescued.

Most recently, more than 27,000 child refugees have fled the Sudanese civil war to come to America. In 2001, three "Lost Boys," as they are called, arrived in the Minneapolis airport one January evening, after a three-day journey from Africa, where they had suffered through homelessness, lion attacks, and tribal wars. Immediately, the boys found themselves in a new world of white faces, overhead lighting, moving walkways, flushing toilets, and blaring televisions.

*The New York Times Magazine* reported that as one of the boys looked out the airport window at the swirling white snow against the dark gray sky, he asked a church caseworker, "Excuse me. Can you tell me, please, is it now night or day?"

## ACKNOWLEDGMENTS

I am deeply grateful to the following people for their contributions to this book:

Edith Westerfeld Schumer
Bruce Jay Wasser
Marian Young
Susan Figliulo
Lisa Graff

Special thanks to editor Melanie Kroupa, who nurtured this work from conception to completion.

# BONUS MATERIAL

# THE STORY BEHIND THE STORY OF THE EDITH/GERDA REUNION

## By Fern Schumer Chapman

"But what happened to Gerda?"

It was the question I couldn't answer—at least, not adequately. So I offered my only honest response: "I don't know."

This brought an exasperated squirm from Jessica Deutsch, one of about eighty middle-school students who had just sat rapt through a talk about my book, *Is It Night or Day?* in the spring of 2011.

After reading the book, Deutsch and her classmates were deeply moved by the friendship of the two twelve-year-old refugees: Edith Westerfeld, who grew up to be my mother, and Gerda Katz, whom Edith met aboard the cruise ship *Deutschland*, which carried them to safety. It was 1938; the girls were alone, their families left behind, and they became friends instantly, playing all day all over the ship, eating all the ice cream they wanted, and bonding over the deep, uprooting loss they shared.

Now, I faced a roomful of skeptical students. They'd read the book; how could the author fail to provide the rest of the story? They buzzed among themselves, shaking their heads.

Jessica Deutsch persisted, a little louder than anyone else. "Haven't you tried to find Gerda?"

"Yes, sure. I've looked online," I said. "But she may have married and changed her name, so I don't even know who I'm looking for." I thought about Gerda's tiny passport photo—all that remained of Edith and Gerda's friendship—a dim, unhelpful picture of a girl with medium-brown hair and a spray of freckles. And I thought of the emotional fragility that has plagued my mother all of her life, and

*1938 passport pictures: Gerda Katz, Edith Westerfeld*

therefore, all of mine. I wasn't about to disturb her ghosts any more than I already had.

Still, I knew the students weren't satisfied with my answer. Neither was my mother, who had been asking me the very same question for years. After reading an early version of *Is It Night or Day?*, she said: "I hope this book is an invitation for Gerda to find me. That's my greatest wish: to see Gerda again."

The girls had parted on March 21, 1938, after the refugee children had been treated to a few dreamlike days in New York City. Then Edith had boarded a train for Chicago while Gerda headed to Seattle, both to join their respective adopted families. They were as lost to one another as to their families back in Germany.

When I began to write about my mother's past, she began to talk, just a little, about Gerda. It was an extraordinary break in the silence she had maintained for years after leaving Germany. "Why is Gerda so important to you?" I asked.

"She is the closest I will ever get to family," my mother answered. Parents, grandmother, aunts, uncles, cousins: every relative she had back home had been murdered in the Holocaust. Even now, seventy years after the genocide, those losses—the people from her past, all of them—beat in her like a second pulse.

How could I make all this clear to the sincerely concerned students of Madison Junior High School in Naperville, Illinois? "The 'girls' are eighty-six-years-old now," I told them, "and I'm not sure if Gerda is even alive anymore. With all the heartbreak in Edith's life, I wouldn't want to have to tell her that sad news, too."

They understood my feelings, but as children of the social-networking age, they couldn't quite imagine why, or even how, anyone would involuntarily be out of touch with anyone else, anywhere in the world. At the very least, they wanted to know what had become of Gerda. They were still talking about it as they returned to their social studies classrooms.

"It's so sad that Edith can't find the one person she can relate to," eighth-grader Meghann Hendricks said. "I can't imagine living without seeing one of my friends for seventy-three years."

"Can't we do something?" Jessica Deutsch pleaded. "Why can't *we* find Gerda?"

Catie O'Boyle, their social studies teacher, was moved by their desire to help and their belief in the possibilities. "Fourteen-year-olds believe anything can be done, and they'll do whatever it takes," Mrs. O'Boyle said. "They are teenagers and they get a bad rap, but they are also extraordinary." Recognizing an opportunity, she agreed to let the students spend a couple of weeks' class time on Gerda's trail.

The students began by researching what they learned was called The One Thousand Children project. Organized by Quaker, Lutheran, and Jewish groups, the project brought children ranging in age from

*Madison Jr. High School Bulletin Board*

fourteen months to sixteen years from Nazi Germany to America. To avoid attention in a climate in America of widespread anti-Semitism, the organization sent just ten children at a time, unobtrusively, on cruise ships. Between 1934 and 1945, the program saved about 100 children a year, ultimately rescuing some 1,200 children. Most of the children's families, the students soon learned, had been killed by the Nazis.

On the very first day of the project, Mrs. O'Boyle's eighth-graders uncovered their first big clue: a newspaper clipping dated April 15,

1939, that listed a Gerda Katz as a member of Girl Scout Troop 43 in Seattle. They soon found another article, this one from the *Seattle Daily Times* of June 10, 1945, listing the graduating class of Garfield High School—including a Gerda Katz. The real breakthrough came a few days later, when students scouring wedding announcements in the *Seattle Daily Times* learned that a Gerda Katz had been married on July 16, 1950. Now that the students knew they were looking for Gerda Katz Frumkin, they could hone their search for more recent news clippings.

A crucial piece of information came from a small community online newsletter, *The Wedgwood Echo,* in which the students found a 2010 article marking the sixtieth wedding anniversary of Perry and Gerda Frumkin. Gerda, the article mentioned, was born in Munzenberg, Germany, and "was sent to America to escape a fate of being sent to a Nazi concentration camp."

As Mrs. O'Boyle read the article out loud, the students let out a collective gasp. "That's it!" one student shrieked, high-fiving the girl next to her. Other students whooped; some got up and danced, "We found her!"

"When we found a possible match," Kyle Jensen recalled, "I was ecstatic. I was awestruck that we actually found the Gerda Katz we were looking for."

To confirm that they had, in fact, found the woman they sought, Mrs. O'Boyle sent Gerda Katz Frumkin this e-mail message on April 23, 2011:

*Mrs. Frumkin,*

*I am really hoping that you are the Gerda Katz we are looking for. We had an author visit our school recently and she told us your story and the story of your friendship with EdithWesterfeld on the* Deutschland *in March of 1938. I have 150 students who are very anxious to hear if you are "our Gerda Katz," as we have come to know her.*

Catie O'Boyle
Social studies teacher
Madison Jr. High School
Naperville, IL

\*   \*   \*

On April 27, after a busy day of speeches on the East Coast, I was scanning my cell phone when I was startled to see a text from a familiar phone number. "Call Me!" it ordered. After seventy-three years in America, my mother remains confused about pronouns, which she believes are sometimes capitalized in English as they are in German. More striking was the fact that this was the first text I had ever received from my mother, who I knew very well did not know how to type on her cell phone. Then I saw she had also sent me an e-mail and left a voicemail repeating the same urgent message. She had covered all her bases while offering no explanation of what this was about.

When I called, she answered the phone with an especially buoyant rendition of her usual "hello."

"Mom," I said. When she heard my voice, she fell silent.

"Mom, what's happened?" For a moment, I began to worry—but her "hello" was still ringing in my ears, and I hadn't heard catastrophe in her greeting.

She gasped and cleared her throat, trying to find words.

"What is it, Mom?" My heart pounded in my ears.

Finally, she managed one word, her voice brimming with the excitement and emotion of a twelve-year-old. "G—G—Gerda," she said.

"What about her?"

"She . . . she . . . wrote me."

She then forwarded me the e-mail she had received earlier in the day.

> *Dear Edith,*
> *I have thought of you often and am so thankful that you*
> *found me. Can't wait until we speak together.*
> *Gerda*

\*       \*       \*

Mrs. O'Boyle's eighth-graders had hoped that Gerda and Edith would reunite at Madison Junior High, but Gerda had been ill and wasn't able to travel to Chicago. Instead, the school invited my mother and me for a day of celebration in early May 2011.

Entering through the school's front doors on a bright, unusually warm day, we stopped before a large glass display case bursting with yellow origami boats—1,000 of them, to be exact. "We made them to represent each of the 1,000 children that America saved," said Jessica Deutsch.

"We folded each of them," she continued. "It took, like, forever. They're all yellow, except ten brown ones that represent the refugee children on the ship that brought Edith to America. The two bright pink ones represent Edith and Gerda and their special friendship."

Arrayed at the back of the library, the school band played a special repertoire prepared for the occasion. To accompany my mother's march into the large, open space—now filled with folding chairs to accommodate the entire school—the musicians enthusiastically squeaked out "My Country, 'Tis of Thee." The trombone player's puffy cheeks were red with effort and moist with tears.

As we approached the two overstuffed chairs set to face the audience, my mother squinted up at a screen displaying a projected image of an elderly woman with short, red hair and a bald-headed man, sandwiching in their embrace a beaming teenager with long, wavy brown hair. "Who's that?" my mother turned to ask me. I had the answer because Mrs. O'Boyle had sent me a copy of the photo earlier that day.

"It's Gerda, her husband, and their granddaughter," I told her.

"Oh, my God!" my mother gasped. The image, I suspect, looked nothing like the picture of twelve-year-old Gerda that Edith had kept in her mind and heart for nearly eight decades. She was just beginning to grasp how these youngsters had changed her world.

Just a few weeks later, in July 2011, my mother got the chance to finally, personally, update that old image. We journeyed to Seattle to meet Gerda and her family, accompanied by a film crew from the Oprah Winfrey Network. Producers at OWN had read about the Madison Junior High students and were here to help orchestrate and capture the reunion of the two women.

Before the dramatic moment of reunion, the crew interviewed Gerda and Edith to explore how each had managed the trauma of her loss and how they felt about seeing each other again. Because I had written two books telling my mother's story, Edith was well-prepared to face her past. "I can't wait," my mother told the OWN interviewer. "This is a dream come true."

Gerda, on the other hand, had coped with her childhood traumas by never telling her family about her early life experiences. When her daughter, Ann Sherman, first asked if she remembered a girl on the ship named Edith, Gerda maintained her carefully constructed wall and emphatically shook her head. But when Ann showed her Edith's twelve-year-old passport picture, Gerda broke down and exclaimed, "*My* Edith!" Memories flooded her; she cried for the next two weeks.

After feeling the full weight of her grief, Gerda decided she was ready to see Edith again. The two would speak—more or less—just once before meeting face-to-face. On the phone, each said hello and then they sobbed together for the next twenty minutes, gasping and moaning, but uttering barely a word.

Edgy and fidgety just before the reunion, my mother, my twenty-year-old daughter, and I waited in a hotel room at the grand Fairmont Olympic in downtown Seattle as the TV production crew organized the timing of the meeting. The three of us didn't say much. None of us, at least not I, dared speak of our fears: Who are these people? What if this is another loss for Edith? Four dreadful words kept running through my head: What have I done?

Finally, the OWN producers called us. My daughter and I escorted Edith into the ballroom, where Gerda was seated on a sofa flanked by her daughter and nineteen-year-old granddaughter. When Gerda first laid eyes on Edith, she jumped out of her seat and both of her arms shot straight up, as if in simultaneous supplication and thanks to the almighty for this answer to her prayers.

"Why didn't you write?" Edith asked as they hugged. For decades, Edith had wondered why Gerda—who had Edith's Chicago address, though she didn't know her own in Seattle—never got in touch after the girls parted.

Gerda, taken aback, said quickly and defensively, "I lost your address."

Edith had interpreted Gerda's silence as another painful abandonment. But with this explanation, she was ready to pick up with Gerda where they had left off. For the next few days, the two women

*2011 reunion in Seattle of Gerda and Edith*

held hands whenever they were together. They sprinkled their conversations with the German they remembered, falling easily back into the inseparable friendship they had established on the *Deutschland* in 1938.

Gerda, we soon learned, had her own amazing family history. Gerda's parents and one brother had escaped Munzenberg, the town where the family had lived for the past 1,000 years, just a week before all Jews in the area were rounded up and taken to concentration camps. Gerda's second brother died in Buchenwald.

What saved the Katzes was a program organized by Rafael Trujillo, the Dominican Republic's brutal dictator, who offered to admit

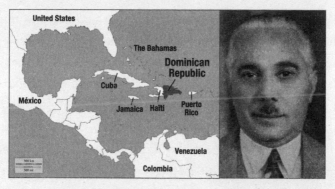

*Dominican Republic Dictator Rafael Trujillo*

100,000 Jewish immigrants at a time when no other nation was willing to take in Jews. Between 1940 and 1945, he issued 5,000 Dominican visas and saved about 3,000 Jews, though of these, only 645, including Gerda's family, settled in his country.

Trujillo welcomed Jews in the hope of "whitening" the Dominican people. The dictator, who used talcum powder daily to lighten his own mixed-race complexion, hoped that young European men would marry native women and produce light-skinned offspring. European Jews, who fled a dictatorship rooted in anti-Semitic hatred, thus found themselves settling in a country whose dictator prized their skin color over that of his own citizens.

The Jews who settled in the Dominican Republic had been professionals or craftsmen in Germany or Austria. Here, each family was given eighty acres of land in the tiny seacoast town of Sosua, along with ten cows, a mule, and a horse. The settlers quickly created businesses, Gerda's family helped run a store that sold sundries, much like the business the family operated in Germany. Other Jewish settlers established Productos Sosua, a cooperative that to this day supplies most of the area's meat and dairy products.

Meanwhile, far away in the United States, Gerda was the first German refugee child to arrive in Seattle. The president of the city's chapter of the National Council for Jewish Women had sponsored Gerda in part to provide a playmate for her daughter, who was five years younger than Gerda.

When she first settled into her new life, Gerda recalled, she didn't know a bit of English. So the principal at her elementary school would call her into his office every day to drill her on vital information.

"He was so afraid I would get lost," she said. "So every day he'd ask me, 'What is your address?' I'd say '1137 32nd Ave.' He'd say, 'What is your phone number?' I'd say, 'Prospect 0667.' Those were my first words in English. I still know my Seattle address and phone number from seventy-three years ago!"

Although Gerda was one of the lucky few whose family was not killed, she would not see her parents again for thirty years. Unable to obtain the necessary exit papers to leave the Dominican Republic, her parents came at last to the United States when they were in their eighties and Gerda in her forties. Her parents were elderly, sickly, and their features had changed with the hot sun and hard life of the tropics. Gerda hardly recognized them.

\*     \*     \*

A few weeks after our trip to Seattle, I asked my mother what it felt like to see Gerda again. "It was like finding my twin," she said. "It was like seeing my mirror image. It helped me understand how our lives were shaped by our childhood losses."

The reunion of Gerda and Edith illustrates what modern kids can teach us—not just about the connective power of technology, but about righting the wrongs of the past. As Mrs. O'Boyle told her students on the day they welcomed my mother and me to their school: "We all know that feeling we have when we first read about the horrors, whether it's what happened to the Native Americans, slavery, or the Holocaust. We feel totally and completely inadequate. We can do nothing," she said, her voice cracking.

"It makes us think we would be better," she said, roping together her fourteen-year-old students with her gaze. "We wouldn't do what they did. But we never have the chance to go back in history and stop it, or be that better person.

"Edith, helping you find Gerda is our way of saying we would never do that." Mrs. O'Boyle stopped, swallowed hard, and then proclaimed, "We would . . . we would stop it."

*Edith and Gerda with the eighth-graders who reunited them*

That conviction resonates deeply with Edith and Gerda. And given what they've rediscovered, both women especially appreciate the technological wizardry of Mrs. O'Boyle's eighth-graders.

Now, twice a week, the two old friends talk on the phone, chatting and laughing, keeping up with each other in minute detail. And when it's time to say good-bye, they conclude each conversation with the same rejoinder:

"You are my sister," Edith purrs into the phone.

Gerda coos back, "And you are my sister."

## Questions for the author
# FERN SCHUMER CHAPMAN

### WHEN DID YOU REALIZE YOU WANTED TO BE A WRITER?

I had a difficult childhood, but writing saved me. I discovered that capturing my emotional life on the page could be therapeutic. As Anne Frank wrote in her diary in April 1944, "I can shake off everything if I write. My sorrows disappear, my courage is reborn."

### WHAT WERE YOUR HOBBIES AS A KID? WHAT ARE YOUR HOBBIES NOW?

Then: Reading, biking, art projects. Now: Reading, biking, art projects.

### WHAT BOOK IS ON YOUR NIGHTSTAND NOW?

I read on my iPad now, so my nightstand is clean. But my iPad bookshelf includes Jeannette Walls, *The Silver Star*; Stephen Grosz, *The Examined Life*; Emma Brockes, *She Left Me the Gun*; and Michael Hainey, *After Visiting Friends*.

I'm also researching adoption issues for my new book, so I'm reading Betty Jean Lifton's *Journey of the Adopted Self* and Nancy Newton Verrier's *Coming Home to Self*.

## WHERE DO YOU WRITE YOUR BOOKS?

I have a home office and I usually write there. But, on cold winter days, I take my laptop and sit in front of the fire.

## WHAT SPARKED YOUR IMAGINATION FOR *IS IT NIGHT OR DAY?*

After a woman read my memoir, *Motherland*, she called and told me that she didn't think I knew about the program that brought my mother to this country. She was right. I didn't know because my mother didn't know. My mother was too young to understand what was happening to her. All she knew was that the Hebrew Immigrant Aid Society (HIAS) had a role in bringing her to this country.

The reader said she thought she could help. She directed me to the One Thousand Children Web site where I first learned about the program that brought my mother to America. As soon as I made this discovery, I realized I could write about my mother's childhood immigration experience. I wanted to raise awareness of this small American program that wasn't mentioned in history books, or even documented in museums. In addition, I wanted to make readers aware of the many children who come to America all alone.

I don't remember the reader's name, but I'd like to thank her for directing me to this path.

## HOW MUCH INVOLVEMENT DID YOUR MOTHER HAVE IN WRITING *IS IT NIGHT OR DAY?*

She answered all of my questions as best she could. But she knew little about the program, and she had shut down her memories in order to cope with her losses. Still, she wanted me to write the book to fulfill a lifelong wish: "I hope this book is like an open letter to my old ship friend, Gerda Katz," my mother said. "I hope Gerda reads this book and finds me. I've thought of her often, and I always wanted to see her again."

## How did she feel about your work researching the One Thousand Children Project?

She was eager to know what I learned. It helped her understand the mosaic of her life. Since this American program was so small and it received little publicity, there wasn't much information about it. In fact, only one book provided original source material: letters, diary entries, and pictures of the One Thousand Children. I relied heavily on that book for details about the childrens' immigrant experiences. In fact, though the book is a work of historical fiction, every story and anecdote in the book came from the experiences of the One Thousand Children.

## How do you think you would have acted in your mother's place?

I like to think that I would be as willing, open, and supportive as she has been of me. I admire her for that, and for her ability to grow and change.

Here's a great example of how this wonderful characteristic presented itself in her ninth decade. Even though she types with two fingers and thinks that only birds "tweet," she recently figured out how to post her first Facebook message on my wall:

> "Dear Fern, Congratulations—Thank You for bringing
> my story to the world. Love Mom"

Note: She still capitalizes the pronoun "you," which is correct German grammar.

### How did knowing what she went through change the way you viewed her?

I felt more empathy for her once I understood her childhood immigration experiences and her profound losses. Now, I appreciate her and love her more deeply. I have a much better understanding of why she struggled with the role of mother.

### Did you have any experiences with immigrants growing up?

Yes. I went to a school that had many immigrant students. Now, I speak at many schools with immigrant populations. My mother's experiences gave me great compassion for these students.

Even though I have written about the challenges, immigration also can be a positive metaphor. In fact, all of us can enlarge our world as "immigrants." I love what writer Jean Rhys said about reading and the immigrant experience. "Reading makes immigrants of us all," she wrote in *Wide Sargasso Sea*. "It takes us away from home, but more important, it finds homes for us everywhere."

### Are you a baseball fan like your mother?

Yes, I like the White Sox but, deep in my heart, I am a long-suffering Cubs fan.

### What was your favorite book when you were a kid?

*Follow My Leader* by James B. Garfield and illustrated by Robert Greiner. In fact, I just ordered another copy of the book. Originally published in 1957, my copy is from the second printing in 1958.

## What's the best advice you have ever received about writing?

Writing should really be called "rewriting."

I love what E. L. Doctorow said about writing a novel: "It is like driving a car at night. You can only see as far as your headlights, but you can make the whole trip that way."

That's how I do it.

## What advice do you wish someone had given you when you were younger?

I wish someone had explained to me that the darkest days are just one snapshot in the photo album of life. Things change quickly. I also wish someone had explained to me that I control what I think.

## Do you ever get writer's block? What do you do to get back on track?

Most writing ideas strike me while I'm riding my bike. That's not surprising given the research that exercise enhances creative thought. For me, biking is a way to stoke my brain. I'm often asked, "Why not use a stationary bike?" Not the same. The combination of exercise and nature feeds me.

Ideas also strike me while I'm driving, walking, even showering, but not with the same frequency or intensity. That's why I am the last biker off the path in December and the first one out in March . . . maybe even February.

## What do you want readers to remember about your books?

My books are about stories, to be sure, but they are much more than that. I would hope my readers understand how deeply I feel about family and history. I want them to know how my mother's experiences defined her, influenced the way she mothered, and, ultimately, shaped the way I see the world. I hope my books inspire readers to learn about their parents and themselves through family history.

As a Jew, I have an obligation to remember and recount. In retelling, even those parts of the past that are painful to relive, I hope to consecrate the memory of those who came before me. In addition, I often recall what Iris Chang, author of *The Rape of Nanking*, said about genocide: "First they kill, and then they kill the memory of killing." I write, in part, so the memory of those who perished and of those who survived the Holocaust endures. I hope to give voice to survivors and refugees who are not capable of telling their own stories.

## WHAT WOULD YOU DO IF YOU EVER STOPPED WRITING?

I'm fascinated with how trauma is transmitted in families. If I stopped writing, I'd love to better understand trauma and study neuroscience.

## WHAT DO YOU CONSIDER TO BE YOUR GREATEST ACCOMPLISHMENT?

Being a loving, steady, present mother.

# *IS IT NIGHT OR DAY?*
# DISCUSSION GUIDE

## CHAPTER ONE: NOBODY TOLD ME ANYTHING

*In 1938, aware of the menacing anti-Jewish atmosphere in Germany, the parents of Edith Westerfeld make preparations to send their youngest daughter to the United States, where Edith will join her sister, Betty, who had departed Germany the year before. The increased discrimination and isolation take a toll on the family, and the young Edith experiences the dual pain of prejudice and fear.*

- Edith said, "We didn't think of ourselves as Jews. We were Germans." What does Edith mean by this statement? How would you describe your own identity?

- While at the synagogue, Edith overheard the adults whispering, "trying to keep details from the young." Have you ever kept a secret from your parents? Why did you not want them to discover what you were hiding?

## CHAPTER TWO: ALL I COULD SEE WAS THE BLUE

*With suppressed emotional anguish, Edith ("Tiddy") departs from her parents on the cruise ship, the Deutschland. A "feeling of sadness" causes her to feel "heavy and dizzy," Edith watches her parents disappear as she departs Germany. She recognizes that her childhood has ended.*

- Imagine yourself in Edith's place. Your family has told you to pack as much of your personal belongings as you can in one suitcase that you will use to start a new life in a new country. What items would you absolutely need to keep with you? What items that are important to you would you have to leave behind?

## CHAPTER THREE: BUT I WANT TO GO TO THE ZOO

*Profoundly dislocated by the abrupt departure from her family, Edith attempts to adjust to life on the* Deutschland. *On board, she meets several children, one of whom will become a steadfast friend. One young boy, traumatized by the experience, cries out that he wants to visit a zoo instead of America. Julius, an older boy who is accompanying his family to America, exudes confidence but makes Edith all the more aware of her predicament. Gerda Katz, a "round, redheaded girl" with "freckles across her nose," emerges as Edith's confidante.*

- Describe a time when a decision your parent(s) made caused you confusion. What have you learned about that decision since your initial confusion?

- Edith is troubled by her perception that her parents "left [her] alone." She spends a great deal of time worrying that she may have done something to cause them to do so. Why does she think this? Is her conclusion right?

## CHAPTER FOUR: SEASICK

*Edith's friendship with Gerda deepens as the two become practically inseparable on board the* Deutschland. *Edith suffers greatly when Julius inquires as to why her parents did not accompany her. "Reminded constantly of that hollow feeling," Edith turns away from the numerous lavish meals offered to passen-*

gers, but develops an insatiable craving for ice cream. An African-American passenger teaches the children a new dance, the Lambeth Walk, an act that arouses suspicion from others aboard the ship.

- The title of the chapter is "Seasick." Although many passengers suffer seasickness, Edith suffers a different type of "sickness." What do you think actually ails Edith?

- When Edith learned how to do the Lambeth Walk, she learned that both the Nazis and even some Americans considered that dance (and jazz music) as "degenerate." What does the word "degenerate" mean?

## CHAPTER FIVE: THIS IS "GOODBYE"

The Deutschland arrives in New York City, and many passengers find themselves deeply moved by the Statue of Liberty and the impressive skyline. Edith meets a stunningly beautiful and confident Jewish chaperone who accompanies the children on a whirlwind three-day tour of the city. Amidst this excitement, Edith must say farewell to her shipboard friends as they disperse themselves across America to new homes. The most painful good-bye is saved for Gerta, who embarks on a cross-country train trip to "Zay-attle."

- Describe a time that you have heard and/or seen a person (it could be yourself) misuse an expression or behave in a manner than marked them as "not quite American."

- While in New York City, Edith goes to a theater and watches a feature Disney cartoon, Snow White and the Seven Dwarfs. She was not prepared for the negative reaction she experienced. Have you ever seen a film that was designed to make you laugh, but instead caused you great worry and/or fear? How is it possible for something designed to be lighthearted to result in sadness?

## Chapter Six: *Willkommen in Amerika*

*Edith boards the* 20th Century Limited, *a train that carries her to her ultimate destination of Chicago. Awkward, frightened, and acutely aware of how out of place she appears, Edith spends time wondering who will meet her at the station. There, she sees her Onkel Jakob—Uncle Jack—an older version of her father. It is a difficult meeting, and Edith cannot hide her disappointment that her sister Betty and her aunt Mildred did not join Jack. Jack gently insists that she remove her identification tag (#108), but that simple act is wrenching.*

- What feelings does Edith experience during the train ride from New York City to Chicago?

- In what ways does Uncle Jack remind Edith of her father?

## Chapter Seven: You Bathe on Tuesdays and Thursdays

*Edith's introduction to her aunt Mildred does not go well. Disdainful of Edith's inability to speak English, Mildred's first words to Edith are: "You bathe on Tuesdays and Thursdays." Edith is further wounded by Mildred's casual dismissal of a letter written by Edith's parents. Even her sister, Betty, appears different, somehow magically Americanized. Edith gradually adjusts to her servant-like status in Uncle Jack and Aunt Mildred's cramped apartment, and Edith suffers the additional indignity of being labeled a "greenhorn."*

- What is your first impression of Aunt Mildred?

- Edith and her sister Betty have an awkward first conversation. Why do you think this is?

# CHAPTER EIGHT: BABY BEAR'S CHAIR

*Edith attends Chicago's O'Keefe Elementary School and finds it a source of alienation, isolation, and humiliation. School officials place the bewildered Edith in a first-grade class, where she sat on a "tiny chair made for six-year olds." On a daily basis, Edith is the focus of the school bullies. Edith refuses to complete a school project on family history. Aunt Mildred quashes any hopes Edith has for friendship with a genuine American girl, Helene Smith. Edith takes solace in the public library, where she feels "safe" and the characters in her books don't "tease" her.*

- How long do you think it takes for an immigrant child to become fluent in English?

- Every day, Edith's class began with the reciting of the Pledge of Allegiance. This made Edith uncomfortable since she didn't understand a word of it and the students' upraised arms looked very much like the Nazi salute. What do you think an immigrant student should do when asked to stand and say the Pledge of Allegiance?

- Uncle Jack gives Edith his treasured German camera, a Leica. What does the camera symbolize?

# CHAPTER NINE: STEP ON A CRACK

*Edith has a difficult time making the transition to her new home. Constantly aware of her parents' absence, she becomes superstitious, convincing herself that if she engages in certain behaviors, her parents would be able to emigrate from Germany. She tries to sell things door-to-door, but the Great Depression has caused practically all of her neighbors to politely refuse her entreaties. Edith describes her growing affection for baseball, particularly the Chicago White Sox. An ominous letter from Edith's mother arrives. In it, Frieda in-*

*forms Uncle Jack that Edith's father has been taken to the Sachsenhausen Labor Camp.*

- Have you ever done chores in your neighborhood for money? What work did you perform and how much did you charge for your services?

- Where is Sachsenhausen? Learn what happened to prisoners who were sent there before World War II.

## CHAPTER TEN: DON'T CALL ME JULIUS!

*Edith receives a letter from Peter. Half out of curiosity and half out of her not-forgotten crush on Julius, Edith sets out to visit him. Dressed in the latest American fashion, Julius is chagrined to see Edith and perturbed at her insistence on using German. Upon her return to the empty apartment, Edith feels a profound loneliness. She sadly concludes that though she lives with her Uncle Jack, Aunt Mildred, and Cousin Dorothy, Chicago is not her home.*

- William Shakespeare asked, "What's in a name?" What do you think Shakespeare meant by that question?

- Think about your own name. What does your name mean? How did you come by your name? Does anyone else share your name? What are your feelings about your name? Do people ever mispronounce or otherwise show disrespect toward your name? Have you ever thought about changing your name?

## CHAPTER ELEVEN: HANKUS PANKUS

*Edith attends her first major league game, at Comiskey Park in Chicago, and has the opportunity to watch her hero, Hank Greenberg of the Detroit Tigers. To Edith, Hankus Pankus is much more than a ballplayer. Contrasted to her* aunt and uncle's relative indifference to being Jewish, "Greenberg was proud to be a Jew and he wasn't afraid to stand up for who he was." When Greenberg connects for a home run, Edith joins the cheering crowd, sensing for the first time the possibility of being both Jewish and American.

- Why do you think Edith takes such a deep interest in Hank Greenberg?

- How important are sports to immigrant children? In what ways do sports help immigrants learn how to become American?

## CHAPTER TWELVE: I TOOK YOU IN

The tension between Aunt Mildred, Dorothy, and Edith reaches a boiling point when Edith returns from Comiskey Park and Mildred orders her to clean up the house after Dorothy's birthday party (to which Edith had not been invited). Despite Mildred's haughty disdain and emotional coldness, Edith acknowledges that Mildred "had done more than most." This causes Edith to reconsider her own definition of family. Eventually, in an act of atonement, Dorothy welcomes Edith into her bedroom and apologizes for her own indifference and cruelties.

- Have your feelings about Aunt Mildred changed since you first met her? Why or why not?

- What is an "epiphany?" What epiphany does Edith have in this chapter? Describe an epiphany you have had in your own life. How did it occur? Did your life change as a result of it?

## CHAPTER THIRTEEN: CHANGE!

Still prepubescent, Edith has a significant conversation with her sympathetic social worker, Mrs. Goldstein. Well aware that she is the "smallest girl" in her class and still has not experienced her monthly period, Edith painfully *acknowledges that she looks "like a child among adults." She agrees with Mrs. Goldstein's suggestion that Edith begin hormone treatments. Shortly after Pearl Harbor, Hank Greenberg returns to active military duty, and Edith receives an official notice that she is to report to the post office and register as an "enemy alien."*

- In a letter, Edith tries to explain baseball to her mother, who has never seen the sport being played. Have you ever tried to explain an activity that you enjoy to a person who knows nothing about it? Were you successful in your explanation?

- Where is Pearl Harbor? What happened there on December 7, 1941, that changed the course of American history?

## CHAPTER FOURTEEN: LABELED

*Edith's sister, Betty, tries to explain the various restrictions that limit both of them as "enemy aliens." Preparing Edith's documents at the post office becomes an ordeal for Edith and Uncle Jack, who has accompanied her. As Uncle Jack helps Edith complete the required forms, Edith sees Julius. They glance at each other, and then Julius quickly averts his eyes in shame.*

- What is an enemy? What is an alien? In your opinion, what exactly is an "enemy alien?"

- Why does Julius turn away from Edith in the post office? Should Edith have walked over and spoken with him?

## CHAPTER FIFTEEN: WHAT DID YOU EXPECT?

*On a beautiful spring day in 1942, Edith returns to the apartment and opens a letter from Mina. The contents stagger Edith. In the letter, Mina tells Edith that her grandmother and parents have died in concentration camps. Aunt Mildred acts irritated when Edith shares this devastating news, responding* with the curt, "What did you expect?" That evening, Uncle Jack shares her grief, confessing his own guilt in not being able to save his brother. Edith senses a profound loneliness with the loss of her parents.

- Explain what Mina means by telling her friend Edith, "We must live."

- What is the symbolism of the Star of David necklace?

## CHAPTER SIXTEEN: WE MUST LIVE

*Edith is filled with shock, anger, and guilt. Emotionally exhausted, Edith is angry with her father for breaking his promise but even more disgusted with herself for not doing enough to save him. By the waters of Lake Michigan, Edith recognizes that her private suffering is but a part of an even greater hurt, one experienced by all who are fighting against the prejudice that decimated Edith's family. She understands that thousands of Americans "were fighting to stop Hitler, fighting so that no more Westerfelds would be murdered. And not one of them even knew my family." She resolves to live.*

- How do you think the United States should honor soldiers who have sacrificed their lives in service to our country?

- Is the conclusion of the novel hopeful or not? What reasons would you give to support your opinion?

---

**Discussion Guide prepared by BRUCE WASSER**

Bruce Wasser served as a public teacher in Newark, California, for over thirty-two years. Honored as Newark's first "Teacher of the Year," Mr. Wasser helped develop "Programs of Conscience" for high school students. These programs encouraged students to develop empathy for those who suffer, and also gave them the courage to protest against prejudice and other social wrongs. For these programs, the California School Board Association honored Mr. Wasser and his colleagues with the prestigious Golden Bell Award.

# Check out these
# Newbery Honor award-winning books!

Available from Square Fish

*The Black Cauldron*
Lloyd Alexander
ISBN: 978-0-8050-8049-0

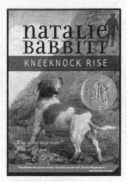

*Kneeknock Rise*
Natalie Babbitt
ISBN: 978-0-312-37009-1

*Abel's Island*
William Steig
ISBN: 978-0-312-37143-2

*Everything on a Waffle*
Polly Horvath
ISBN: 978-0-312-38004-5

*The Surrender Tree: Poems of
Cuba's Struggle for Freedom*
Margarita Engle
ISBN: 978-0-312-60871-2

*Joey Pigza Loses Control*
Jack Gantos
ISBN: 978-0-312-66101-4

*Find out more about*

# IS IT NIGHT
# OR DAY ?

**DISCOVER THE LATEST FROM THE AUTHOR**

fernschumerchapman.com

**DOWNLOAD THE COMMON CORE—ALIGNED DISCUSSION GUIDE**

us.macmillan.com/isitnightorday/FernChapman